The Wandering Albatross

The Wandering Albatross

Richard Inwood

The Wandering Albatross

& other stories

The Wandering Albatross & other stories
ISBN 978 1 76109 262 6
Copyright © text Richard Inwood 2022

First published 2022 by
GINNINDERRA PRESS
PO Box 3461 Port Adelaide 5015
www.ginninderrapress.com.au

Contents

First Voyage

Hugh Stanley stepped out of the compartment at Dover and looked at his first ship, just glimpses of it through the arches of the station building. There it was, beyond the tracks, a section of black hull and a double line of rivets, white handrails and varnished doors: a solid section of ship that very slowly lifted to the gentle heave of the harbour swell and raised the near handrail, so that it was silhouetted against the cold sky with its high-flying clouds.

He stood motionless with his heavy leather suitcase at his feet, a blue gabardine raincoat over his arm: like an island pressed all around by the tide of urgent, forward-leaning people, their eyes aiming ahead, faces stamped in the holidaymakers' mould. For them, the sight and smell of the sea and squeal of gulls was an assurance that this was the start of their thrills, crossing the Channel to the other side, but for him it was the uncertain, exciting step into a new life.

Three thousand tons, nineteen knots, six thousand horsepower, two trips a day, three hundred passengers each way. She'd been a command ship during the Normandy invasion, and here, five years later, she was back on the trade, still looking proud and immaculate. All the details were in his head. This is what he'd worked for, and the uniform he wore, with the two wavy lines of gold braid on his coat sleeve, the officer's cap with its Merchant Navy badge, all from Harvey's, and the new discharge book in his pocket, were legitimate credentials for his entry into a life of ships and the sea.

An icy wind hissed across the wharf and slapped him in the chest. He felt the warmth of his armpits go cold and had the urge to urinate.

He lifted the suitcase and joined the stream of people heading for the customs barrier, a young man of twenty-one with clean, even features and blue eyes, eyes that held shadowy reflections of doubt. But in the way he kept his lips firmly pressed and held his head there was the hint of a fledgling personality, which though as yet untested was nevertheless predisposed towards determination.

His thoughts were fleeting, darting excursions, searching for relief from the overwhelming grip of uncertainty that held his mind captive. The saving thought came that he'd often felt this way before, and it hadn't been that bad after all. He was erect, with a controlled look on his face, and in an effort to still the turmoil inside him, he looked fixedly ahead, giving an unhurried appearance.

The voices and contact of shuffling, winter-clothed bodies all around him formed a background to his thoughts, and despite his preoccupation still made inroads, as he felt a nudge, or heard the harassed voice of a parent, the laughter of a girl, and he was conscious of the quick, bright smiles he received: a cross-section of the British public, heavy-shouldered rednecked men, tall fur-clad women, pert girls with silken hose and woollen sweaters over thrusting breasts, the collars of their top coats framing their cheeks. Lovely. All this was new too and part of the mystery.

He came through the barrier onto the wharf. The entire ship was visible now, tied fore and aft to the stumpy black bollards. As he walked down its length, the near side of the ship moved up and then slowly sank back again, squeezing the large fenders between it and the wharf. Before going aboard, he put the suitcase down at the foot of the gangway and worked his fingers to restore the circulation.

A seaman in a turtlenecked sweater stood at the top. 'Number two Sparks?' he queried.

Hugh nodded.

The seaman went forward, expecting to be followed, down the outer passageway, up some stairs amidships, emerging on the main deck just aft of the bridge. 'Here we are,' he said, opening a heavily varnished door.

'Thank you,' Hugh commented. On the basis of some instinct he found himself being brief and noncommittal. Polite, that's all. It seemed the right thing to do.

He stripped down to the waist and washed his face and neck in an effort to freshen himself and overcome the first feeling of discomfort that was prompted by the last heave of the ship. The soapy water in the basin took on a slant and his gabardine on its hook swung away from the bulkhead. Quickly he put on a clean shirt, slipped his coat on and stepped outside into the fresh air.

He located the radio room by glancing up and following the aerial down-lead to the main insulator. He knocked on the door, pushed it open and was faced by a man of medium height, wearing glasses. His uniform had a well-worn sheen to it and the two wavy lines of gold braid on the sleeve, with the diamond between them were dull with years of service.

'Hello, hello,' he said, standing up with a quick movement. He crushed a cigarette to death with a deliberate twist of his spatulate fingers and blew a cloud of smoke down his front, flapping at the ash that had smudged his lapel. Light flashed from his glasses. 'Palmer.' He held out a thick, stumpy hand.

The pips came out of a radio receiver and a BBC announcer started reading the coastal forecast. Palmer held up his hand. He was sallow-faced, with a dry, lustreless skin, and his broken teeth were aired when he drew his lips back in a dubious smile.

'Moderate to rough. Thirty knots. Not bad.' He cocked his ear to the barely audible creak that came with the heave of the ship. 'First trip. Do you get seasick?'

'Yes, I suppose so. Does she roll much?'

'Like a sow. Don't muck around. Stick your finger down and dredge it up, lumps and all.' Behind his spectacles, his brown eyes had a liquid, protuberant and shifty expression.

Hugh looked at the mass of radio equipment. Very different to what he'd worked on at the wireless college.

The bulkhead creaked again.

Palmer inclined his head towards the gear. 'Different, what? No matter, all very simple.' For the next few minutes, he went through all the procedures. 'Go on,' he enthused, 'give Northforeland, GNF, a burst. We're GJQY.'

Hugh used the up and down key and made the call. GNF came back straightaway, and for the first time a slow smile spread across his face.

'Do you drink?' Palmer broke in.

'Not much. A beer once in a while.'

'I'll buy your gin issue off you. A pity you smoke. Good price on the other side.' He ran the palms of his hands flat against the side of his head and smoothed his hair down. 'Let's go topside and see the crumpet come aboard.'

When they were on the main deck and leaning over the railing, he rubbed his hands together, as though in anticipation. 'Nippy, isn't it,' and then in the same breath, 'Look at that one in the green!.' He hissed between his teeth as if suffering some exquisite pain.

Hugh looked at the throng below with pretended interest. He began to feel unwell, clutching the cold railing as each incoming swell lifted the ship. The motion was very slight and he began to despair when he thought how it would be outside

For about five minutes, Palmer kept up a running commentary. He glanced quickly at Hugh. 'You look a bit seedy. Go on, have a short kip. Come down when we get underway.'

Hugh had hardly lain down when there was a knock and a tubby, red-faced man came in, wearing the chief mate's stripes. He was round-faced, with bright blue eyes and looked like a younger version of Charles Laughton.

'Hello, Sparks. How's everything?'

'Not too bad, sir. A bit seedy.'

'No need to call me sir, that's only for Tiger, the skipper. First time, what! You'll probably spew your ring up. Clears the liver. D'you drink?'

'The chief RO's already asked me.'

'I'll double it.'

Hugh shook his head. 'Sorry, I've already told him.'

'Well, can't be helped. A pity you smoke. A carton does wonders on the other side. Hang onto your laundry soap.' He paused. 'You'll have to meet the skipper. I'll get the second mate to take you up. I suppose Palmer's perving, as usual,' he said before ducking out.

Hugh lay back and closed his eyes. He tried to collect his thoughts and a quick wave of loneliness swept through him. He was helpless in the grip of a nauseous feeling, his senses alert to the barest motion of the ship, the soughing of the wind outside and the smell of paint and varnish. He was new and acutely aware of the difference between himself and the men he'd met. Never had a girl, never had a drink of gin. He'd been aboard barely an hour, and so far he'd met a scruffy seaman and two officers, both black marketeers, one a sex maniac and the other a gin soak.

It was hopeless trying to rest. He went out on deck, going to the windward side and allowing the icy wind to chill his skin. High above, the gulls hung motionless with wings slightly furled, now and then emitting plaintive cries. He heard a voice behind him and swung round to look into the smiling face of the second mate. His hand was cupped over the bowl of his pipe, protecting it from the gusts. They both turned and walked to the other side, being pushed by the wind.

'Jack Ellis,' he said and held out his hand. He sucked on his pipe. 'Let's go up to the holy place and see the captain. Don't worry,' he smiled, 'he'll probably just nod.'

Hugh could feel the chill of the handrail as he climbed the steps leading to the wing of the bridge, a chill that was matched by the cold around his ribs.

This was holy ground and the sound of the steps was deadened by the rubberised matting as they walked towards the large man out on the wing. He was looking at the crowd on the wharf and turned as they approached. A big, bulldog of a man with a red, heavy-jowled face and a dark shadow over his bulging jaws, where the closest of shaves had failed to hide the impatient thrust of his beard. His watery blue eyes challenged them briefly from under dark, bristling brows and his whole face was a stern, almost brutal mask of power under the shadow of his cap with the gold, scrambled eggs on the peak of it. Four rings of gold braid on his coat sleeves and the treble row of faded rainbow-hued war ribbons were symbols of authority and courage, and by the malevolent look in his eye, it appeared that he detested the humdrum, routine things of life.

'Sir,' Ellis said, 'the new second RO.'

The captain looked at Hugh with a deliberate, yet uncomprehending glance. He was a man vastly experienced, weathered and moulded into an impregnable, unfeeling fortress of strength, incapable of allowing softness to erode the foundations upon which his character had been built. Tiger. Thirty years at sea separated the two, and it was too great a gap to cross with anything but the barest of nods.

'That's it,' Ellis commented when they were on the deck below. He tapped his pipe into the cupped palm of his hand. 'Don't try to take it all in at once. How d'you feel?'

'Not good. How long does the crossing take?'

'A couple of hours. Straightforward pitch, punching into it. A roll or two maybe.'

From the bridge they heard the flat 'tring' of the wheelhouse telegraph being tested, and almost immediately the muted response coming up through the engine-room ventilator.

'I'd better get aft,' Ellis said. 'Calais tonight and here tomorrow.' He paused. 'Come and have dinner with us. Meet the wife.'

The whistle gave a short, peremptory blast causing an added spurt to the activities on board and on the wharf. From the passenger deck below, the babble of sound was interspaced with small excited shrieks and thump of hurrying feet.

The seagulls hovered anxiously aft, waiting for the churn of propeller blades and the bubbling, frothy swirl of water full of minute harbour debris. The centre and aft gangways were removed and cries of farewell were shouted back and forth.

Hugh was standing directly below the bridge, looking at the crowd. He felt strangely detached from the emotional display down there. He was not part of it, untouched by the excitement of departure and pathos of farewell, the shining eyes and parted lips. A lone figure placed in the unenviable no-man's-land of change, in mid-step and about to cross into a new experience: poised with the slate scrubbed clean and waiting for the new term to begin: the seconds to step out of the ring, or the cavalry to charge, and then he thrilled to the first words of command issued in heavy, even tones from the bridge. 'Let go forward. Let go aft.' The metallic cackle of the engine telegraph and the throb of the engine through the soles of his shoes.

Suddenly he smiled, as though triggered from inside. He felt the sudden release of pent-up feelings, sweeping away away all doubts and as the bow swung away from the wharf he leaned over the railing and searched for a pretty face. He found one on the edge of the throng, and as their eyes met, he waved and was rewarded by a smile and wiggle of fingers from a slender, gloved hand. Elated, he turned away and walked purposefully towards the radio room, buoyed by a feeling of invincibility and eagerness for things to begin.

The bow lunged into the heavy swell at the harbour entrance and was instantly claimed by the eager heave and pull of confused seas. It rose sharply upwards, as if shocked by the touch of the green, icy water. In its climb, it seemed to bound over the onrushing crests, pushed by the propeller astern, and then just as sharply it knifed down into a trough, was smacked wetly by a muscular cross swell and shouldered aside, buried by a high-reaching crest which creamed over the forecastle, and then rose again with a mane of white-water trails streaming from the scuppers and anchor flukes.

Hugh's eyes had that glazed and tortured look that comes with the holding of one's breath for a long time, as though the relentless force that held him had drained his will to live and was daring him to breathe. He was at the top of a stairway with a railing hard against his stomach, bent over it and looking down the flight of steps to the deck below, shoved there rudely by the final lurch. He swallowed heavily, holding back the well-digested mass of egg, toast and breakfast cereal that bubbled thickly in the column of his throat, flung up by an outraged stomach.

'God!' he whispered. It was like a prayer that found its amen in the moan of misery that came from those unfortunates who, like him, had been caught unawares, flattened against bulkheads, down in heaps in disarray, lesser beings, held tightly in the grip of nausea and all, without exception, praying for relief.

The sound of breaking crockery from the dining saloon gave him a small measure of satisfaction, and though of dubious texture it was the first emotion to escape from the seal behind which the total misery of his thoughts and actions had been frozen, behind which his wail had been trapped. He lurched his way to the radio room and with a sick smile of relief wedged himself in the doorway, mustering his reserves for the next few steps

'Ah,' Palmer said brightly, 'made it. Here we are. Stand by for the rush.' He stepped to the intercom and announced that telegrams were now being accepted for all destinations. He turned round beaming and saw the look on Hugh's face. 'No. Not in here. Not on the gear!' He gave Hugh a shove. 'Across the passageway!'

Hugh had a hand clamped over his mouth. He propelled himself across to the toilets in a race to beat the warm, alive mass nudging wetly against his palm, and when with the next two giant strides he came within range, he was no longer his own master. Like some tortured creature, bent over, hot and cold, red in the face, neck-cords taut and with jaws agape, he felt a projectile of vomit hiss lumpily past his teeth into the white, sympathetic bowl, feeling the wretched heave of his stomach and spasms of the anal sphincter. Down he went on his knees, racked and beaten, wrung dry, taking deep gasping breaths, eyes swimming with tears, with a red-raw throat and spittle on his chin, down by the toilet bowl with his arms lovingly around it.

When he stood up, he felt like a new man, weak but alive. He rinsed his mouth, splashed water on his face and opened a port for a breath of fresh air. He made a quick, almost furtive return to the radio room, conscious of his colourless face and strained, bloodshot eyes.

'Lovely,' Palmer said. 'Does your liver good.' He waved a handful of messages. 'The rush hasn't started yet. All the breathless young things will send telegrams, a load of rubbish, plus a dowager or two. They'll try to tip you. They do it on the Frog side all the time. They think you're a waiter. Refuse. Officer, y'know.' He sat down and started tuning up. 'You man the counter and I'll do the sending. Vice versa on the way back. Good steady stuff.'

Hugh reached for a half bottle of tonic water. 'Can I have this?'

'Sure, get it down you.'

He gargled briefly, puffing out his cheeks, swallowed the rest and felt the fresh, tingling sensation around his teeth and gums.

The ship punched into a wave, rolled sharply to port and stayed there for many long seconds, longer than necessary before coming back to an even keel.

'God!' Palmer shouted, 'that QM on the wheel needs to be shot!'

Hugh did a couple of dry retches and felt a clamminess on his forehead.

'Streak through the door if you feel it coming on…STEADY…' Palmer yelled in a long drawn-out cry as the ship rolled again, 'Ah, here we are. Customers.'

Hugh stepped to the counter and began accepting messages, counting and charging each one carefully, nervous about giving the wrong change, but gradually gaining confidence as he glanced up into smiling faces, answering their polite questions and whiffing their perfumes: mouths phrasing earnest questions through the grillwork, the occasional heavy-jowled face and tobacco-stained teeth clamped around a pipe stem; the soft, genteel voice of a grey-haired matron. All of them radiating their personalities in varying degrees.

Behind him the dit dit dit dah dit of Palmer's Morse, giving GNF hell, sending batches of ten, on and on until an hour later the numbers were approaching the hundred mark. Then suddenly, one by one, the various dimensions of the whole busy scene disappeared, as the hiss of high-flung spray died away and each roll became more gentle, and once again he could hear the throb of the engine.

'That's it,' Palmer said over his shoulder and broke into Hugh's thoughts. 'Calais, m'lad,' and without pause he continued to send the still substantial pile of traffic. 'The train will have choofed off, halfway to Paris and I'll still be ploughing through this.'

The ship was almost motionless now and it seemed that they were the only two below. There was a slight bump, and he heard the faint, final ring of the engine telegraph.

'Five more,' Palmer announced. 'We'll go whoring tonight!'

'I don't know,' Hugh said dubiously.

Palmer's sending suffered as he screwed up his face and winced. He stopped in the middle of a message, about to say something, but continued to pound the key while shaking his head.

That evening, Hugh placed his feet on French soil. He had the sensation that the ground was moving, almost as though it was breathing. His first trip was over. He wondered what lay ahead.

Kids

We got to the Arno Bay caravan park in the late afternoon, with plenty of time to set ourselves up. It all looked good. A clear blue sky and a calm sea, and the long jetty was only about forty metres away. We'd have fresh fish for dinner for sure.

We chose a good spot against a scrub-covered sand dune, which dipped down to a narrow beach. We'd be lulled to sleep with the hiss and sigh of the waves running in.

There was only one blemish. There was the sound of shouting, shrieking kids. It was an affliction to my ears, spoiling a good atmosphere. I began muttering to myself.

'What's the problem?' My wife said. She eyed me as I drew a cask of claret out of a bottom cupboard.

'The shouting. They're only a foot away from each other!'

'They're just kids, enjoying life. It's what kids do,' she interrupted. As an ex classroom teacher, she knew all about them.

I was in the seventy-plus years of age cocoon, and comfortable in it. Having weathered the passage of time, of life, I felt I had the right to choose my comfort zone. Shouting kids, even my own grandchildren, were not welcome in the envelope. I let it pass. No doubt the parents were sucking on tinnies, listening to the footy and firing up the barbecue.

Using maggots, I caught half a dozen good-sized tommies, enough for dinner. Other fishers were trying for squid with minimal results, always hopeful: there were scores of ink splotches on the jetty as proof that others had had better luck. It was what fishing was all about. Hope.

For the next few days, I continued fishing for tommies and always had enough for a meal. The reason I hadn't tried catching squid was that I didn't know how to handle them. There was an art in removing the innards, the head, the feathers, wings and so on.

Anyhow, one evening I set up a squid rig, using a green lure. It was quite late in the evening and a bit cool as I got to the jetty and met a couple of adults, just leaving. They hadn't had much luck and complained about two youngsters who had spent most of their time running up and down shouting. I could hear their voices at the end of the pier. When I got there, I saw two what I considered ferals, kids of about ten or eleven, disappearing down wooden stairs that led to the water's edge, hurling objects at the cormorants that were sheltering under the pier. There was much shouting and cursing as they scored near misses.

They checked me out and I checked them out, as if we were the first contacts of hostile tribes. Their bicycles were leaning against the railings. They made a cursory check of their squid floats and I saw them go to a milk crate tied to the carrier of one of their bicycles. It held bits and pieces of chopped-up fish, snapper heads, damaged tommies and mullet. They grabbed three or four each and excitedly ran towards the pier. They began to hurl their projectiles, shouting at the top of their voices and then rising to a cheer as they scored a direct hit. The stunned bird flapped for a few metres and then took off towards a safer haven.

I was getting annoyed at the noise, exacerbated by a feeling of frustration. Putting it simply, I didn't know what to say to them. Heck! I didn't know how to handle a squid, or to speak to kids. How d'you do that these days? How do you question their behaviour? Apart from giving a bellow of rage!

They returned to their fishing gear, still pumped up with the success of their last attack, jabbering away, and then rushed to one of their lines, the float of which was bobbing up and down. They hauled in a squid that expelled clouds of ink in the trauma of its capture, with a final squirt as it landed on the pier. One of them stooped down and very deftly twisted the head off and then, with fingers that knew what to do, quickly removed bits and pieces here and there and ended up with a clean white tube. Having done that, they restarted their cormorant attack and the noise continued.

As dusk approached, flights of cormorants began arriving in batches, looking for night-time shelter. It was what the boys were waiting for, as if they were manning machine guns on the deck of a warship, blazing away at low-flying kamikaze aircraft. There were splashes, shouts, confusion, more shouts and curses galore.

For a brief moment, I remembered my childhood days, when armed with a catapult or airgun, I fired at anything that moved: squirrels, crows, hawks. I must have gone into a daydream.

'Mister…you've got one!'

I quickly looked at my float and it was very agitated.

'Quick. Pull it in, it's a bewdy,' one of the lads said excitedly.

I hauled away and up it plopped on the jetty, squirting ink. They looked at me and I at them.

I gave a sort of shrug and after a moment I said, 'I've never caught one. I suppose you're full bottle on what to do?'

They looked at me wide-eyed. 'Easy,' they said.

We all hunkered down above the poor creature.

The younger lad became the instructor. He removed the lure from the tentacles. 'First you take the head off, you see,' and he twisted the head away from the body and in a conversational tone he continued, 'You see, clear away all the slime and using our thumbs ease the wings away, pull them off, you can eat them or use them for bait, then dig in here and grab the feather, see, pull away from the slime and then pull the guts,' and then he inserted a finger and pulled the tube inside out.

'Very good,' I said. 'Thanks.'

'If you catch another, I'll show you.'

I chucked my lure out and a few minutes later I caught another. The lads came over quickly.

'See, pull the head off, then the wings,' and the younger one went through the whole procedure.

'You're an expert,' I said.

'Nah, we're just used to it.' He looked me in the face. 'What's your name?'

'Dick,' I said.

He nodded. 'Dick,' he repeated. 'I'm Chris and this is Peter.'

'All those fish,' I nodded towards the crate. 'Where did you get those?'

'Rejects…from our dads. They're fishermen.'

'Would you like a squid,' I offered.

'Nah, nah, we've got plenty, Dick.'

It was getting quite dark and the jetty lights came on. 'I think I'll try for tommies now,' I said.

'Now's the best time,' they both agreed. I brought in four nice tommies in the next ten minutes and decided to call it a day.

'I think I'll pack it in.' I said to them.

'Yeah, we'll go home soon.'

I walked back to the caravan park to the fish cleaning shed, located at the start of the jetty. It was a good set-up. A cement floor with drains, a Besser block waist-high wall, galvanised troughs, lights, and all under cover. There was also a cleaning board and a two-forty-litre bin for scales, fish heads and guts.

I was busy cleaning the fish when I heard them cycling up in the dark.

They stopped near the shed and I heard the younger one, Chris, say to Peter, 'That's Dick. D'you think we should give him a hand?'

'I dunno. He's doing all right. Tommies are easy.'

'Hey, Dick, d'you want a hand?' Chris called.

'No thanks, cobber,' I said. 'Thanks, just a bit more to do.'

'Okay, Dick, we'll see you again,' Chris said.

'Sure, ' I said. 'Thanks, Chris. Thanks, Peter. Goodnight.'

I went back to the caravan with the cleaned tommies and two squid tubes. My wife was quite impressed. I poured myself a glass of claret and told her about the two boys. She smiled as I described what had happened. I felt good about it all.

'There you are,' she said. 'Those two young kids will remember you, and you'll remember them…friends for life.'

Lost in the Jungle

I was a product of the Indian Plains and lower Himalayan regions. Boyhood activities involved hunting, shooting and fishing, always with a gun in my hand. Experiences of the past always linger and as the years advanced taking me into manhood and other paths of life, I often reflected on distant memories.

Way back in 1961, newly married, my wife Annette and I arrived in Port Moresby, Papua New Guinea, with an open-ended contract of employment with a communication company. This was in the days of Morse code.

We settled in nicely, with a comfortable house close to a beach and waving palm trees. As was customary, we employed a local 'house boi', a young Rigo man named Qualim, and formed a good bond.

We bought a Peugeot 403 and began exploratory trips into the bush and jungle, using very primitive roads, beyond the Laloki and Vanapa rivers down the Brown River road. The jungle here was very dense, barely allowing room to move, three-tiered with undergrowth pushing up trees that reached for the sky hundreds of feet high, just allowing dappled sunlight to filter down. It was a massive ecosystem, hundreds of square miles in extent, virtually unspoilt and harbouring insects, snakes, birds, wallabies, wild pigs, iguanas, jungle fowl, and goura pigeons. Swamps in the forest held crocodiles, giant perch, tilapia, barramundi and eels, fed by the rivers nearby.

I was at this time regrettably still at the stage where my hunting, killing instincts had not been sublimated by the purer motives of conservation. It was hard to deny the habits of an entire adolescent period, gun in hand on the Indian Plains. I was eager to try the New Guinea jungle.

With Annette, Qualim, shotgun and ammunition, I set off, drove for an hour, crossed the Laloki and Brown, onwards and turned down a rudimentary forest track which sent a spur into the jungle and came to a dead end. While Annette and I were heavily shod, Qualim was barefooted, dependent on the hard leather of his soles for protection, and a T-shirt and lap lap completed his outfit. Though he was a Rigo and a savannah native, the jungle would be no stranger to his natural instincts, which I conceded would be better honed than mine in this environment. In fact, I felt dependent on it.

We locked the car door and walked into the undergrowth, with me leading and scanning the immediate area ahead for reptiles. The undergrowth got thicker and began to drag at our knees and hips. There was the muted sound of wind through the branches hundreds of feet up, the swaying and rustling and sounds of birds close by and distant.

I tried to keep a mental picture of our progress and of the reverse track we'd have to do to return to our starting point. I felt safer having Qualim with us. It was oppressively hot and steamy though only ten o'clock in the morning. Looking up through the middle jungle with its tangled foliage, it was difficult to get an accurate fix of where the sun was, diffused as it was by dappled light in a massive mesh of green.

We heard the raucous cackle of a jungle fowl and Qualim pointed a finger. I could have sworn it came from another direction, deceived by its ventriloquism. We began to track the sound, stepping silently, crouched low, with Annette hanging onto my trouser belt. The fowl was close, emitting cackles of alarm. I crouched even lower and got a brief glimpse of the fowl, about the size of a bantam hen, about thirty feet away. I fired the right barrel using number 4 shot and rushed forward. There was no bird. It was unbelievable to have missed. In that millisecond between sighting and pulling the trigger, the bird must have launched itself, escaping the close-grouped charge. I searched but found nothing.

I figured Qualim was searching further ahead. 'D'you know where he is?' I asked Annette.

She shook her head.

'Qualim?' I called.

Silence.

'Qualim?' I called, much louder.

We looked at each other, hot and sweaty. I kept calling his name, as loudly as I could. Minutes went by and a thought entered my mind that we were alone, in an area alien and vast. It also came to me that Qualim could also be lost. I raised the gun barrel and fired a couple of shots. Silence, just the whisper of the leaves. After several minutes, I fired another round.

I took Annette's hand. 'We have to go back.' I pulled her close and enveloped her in a feeling of intense love.

A terrible sadness came over me as I looked at her, just twenty-one. We'd only been married a few months. What had I done? There was a sense of panic, and options flooded my mind. Stay where we were, or move. The danger was that we could go in circles. We were about half a mile into a sea of jungle and we'd have to find the spur we'd started from.

We turned and made our first steps, looking for undergrowth that could show our previous passage but it closed up behind us. We continued calling to Qualim and firing shots. We'd pause, mouths open, listening for any sound, even the distant passage of a car on the Brown River road but all we could hear was our heavy breathing. It was midday and our thirst was increasing. Were we going in the right direction, should we deviate to the right or left? A thought fled through my mind, a memory of something I'd read about a New Zealander who had been lost in this very jungle and never found. The opinion of the experts had been that when weak and exhausted, the wild pigs would have got him. I also remembered advice to stay away from swamps and rivers and the threat of crocs. I would have welcomed a river to assuage our thirst.

We blundered on and as we moved the jungle closed in behind us. We pushed forward ten feet, turned to look back, and there as not a hint of our passage. By three in the afternoon, we were in a state of despair, very thirsty and with tongues slightly swollen. We silently acknowledged that we were completely lost. Wordlessly, we held each other.

As we stumbled through the undergrowth, we disturbed several groups of wallabies, the small forest dorcopsis variety. They hurtled between us in fright, one passing between Annette's legs. Some time later, I heard the grunt of pigs. I can't imagine how many snakes and lizards had slithered away at our approach. A flight of cranes flew low over the jungle canopy, honking as they went. It meant that a swamp was possibly a few miles away.

Totally, utterly lost, exhausted, thirsty and in the depths of despair, our brains shrouded in a dark shadow of fear. Within ten miles of us there was water, the Brown and Laloki rivers and the vast Waigani swamp but in no way attainable.

Even at noon, down on the forest floor it was dim, and as it came up to five o'clock, it began to get dark. We came to a halt beside a large tree and sank down at its base. We were in a lather of sweat, hands and arms scratched. We had both picked up several leeches and I plucked them off as Annette averted her eyes, They were plump with the blood they'd sucked.

I took stock of our situation. I had about fifteen shotgun cartridges left, all number 4s, enough for pigs at close range, but I doubted they'd try anything until they sensed we were too weak. We could survive the horrible night, despite our thirst, but the long hours of darkness, the mosquitos and mental anguish would take their toll and the morning would find us a lot weaker. If it rained, we had a chance and I sent a prayer up, Dear God! I had matches and could light a fire, which would give us some comfort and at least drive mosquitos away. My heart bled for Annette. She had not complained once, no recrimination, not a whimper.

I began to prepare the area around the tree, clearing branches and sweeping away leaves, pulling at creepers and making a clean area, free of vegetation, mainly to keep leeches away. I paused for a moment and looked up. I saw a glint in the distant gloom. I saw it again, a flicker, and my legs began to move and in an instant I was like a charging animal pushing through the undergrowth, fighting to close the gap towards the glint.

I gave a hoarse cry, coming from a raw, dry throat and a swollen tongue and I saw a movement and then the shape of a Papuan native. He stood stock-still, a look of alarm on his face at the sight of a charging, shouting white man, a *taubada* with a gun. Quickly, he unlimbered his shotgun which lay across his shoulder, letting two dead wallabies slide off the barrel. It was the glint of the gun. Immense relief filled my chest and I felt Annette behind me, breathing hard, stumbling against me.

Thank God I knew a few words of Motu, which I'd been studying. Road was Dara. 'Dara, Dara!' I blurted out the words over and over.

The man understood, nodding and pointing ahead. Thank God, we had a life. There was no emotion on his face, just an unblinking stare, taking in a picture of white people in an emotional state of distress.

He moved forward silently, weaving his way through the undergrowth on what to him was a well defined path, a saviour in a pair of torn khaki shorts, bare-chested, with a pair of glazed-eyed wallabies hanging from the end of his single-barrel shotgun.

It was a good hour as we stumbled behind him before the jungle ceased suddenly and there in the dark was the road. Our salvation. I gave him the only thing I had of value. All the ammunition and the bandolier I was carrying, with about ten cartridges. We were rewarded by a smile, showing his betel-stained teeth. Impulsively, I grabbed his hand. He nodded and quietly went back into the forest.

We began to walk slowly down the road, terribly tired, arms around each other, barely able to talk. No moisture in our mouths. Raging thirst. We'd been going since ten in the morning. The lights of a car a long way off gave us the long-awaited hope. It was the Brown River road, dead straight, and it took ages to come close. It was a utility with a white man in the driver's seat, with a Papuan woman beside him. He rolled down his window and saw our dishevelled state and asked us what had happened. I detected a Dutch accent. A Dutchman and his native wife.

'Water, water please,' I said.

He immediately took the top off two lemonade bottles, which Annette and I grasped with shaking hands. It was glorious as the liquid filled our mouths. Despite the urge, we were careful to avoid gulping it down. We gave him the story and he opened another bottle.

'Very, very lucky man, you too, missus,' he said solemnly, shaking his head. He owned a trade store near the Vanapa River.

We clambered aboard in the back and he drove slowly down the road looking for the spur we'd followed into the jungle. We came to it a few miles further, closer to the Laloki, turned down it and after half a mile there was the car, and beside it Qualim. When he saw us, he began to cry, unashamedly, tears running down his face. He grabbed our hands. It was too much and we began to bawl. Qualim then spoke rapidly to the Papuan woman, who nodded repeatedly and then translated. Evidently, he had gone to the main road and stopped several cars, telling the drivers that his Taubada and Sinabada were lost and to tell the police. As it later turned out, no one had done so.

We gave our heartfelt thanks to the Dutchman and his wife and said goodbye. I turned the ignition on, heard the engine come to life and headed back towards Moresby, to safety, to life, food, water and a bath.

We lay in the still of the night, silent, thinking, going back to our lucky escape. With the moonlight casting its softness through the slatted louvres, we listened to the waves lapping on Ela Beach, the flapping of flying fox wings outside and the gentle whirr of the overhead fan. We were fairly certain that our son, Richard, was conceived that night.

Chloe

The *Tawi Tawi* sailed from Greenock, Scotland, on her maiden voyage, heading for distant Hong Kong. For the first time, her bows would feel the open sea, the chilly Bay of Biscay and eventually the temperate waters of the Yellow Sea.

I was also on my maiden voyage to the Far East: a long haul to Australia, via Capetown. It was exciting. We'd go up the east coast of Australia, through the Barrier Reef and the Arafura sea, and finally reach Hong Kong.

The second mate, Sandy Wilson, and I soon became friends. He had been at sea for a couple of years, on the West African coast. He was twenty-three and I had just turned nineteen. I was the radio officer. Sandy more or less took me under his wing like an older brother. He was short, about five-eight, but broad-shouldered and solidly built. He had unruly hair, a ready smile and mischievous brown eyes under bushy eyebrows. Like me, he was looking forward to seeing Australia, with its fabled beaches and bronzed, long-limbed girls.

We stopped at Fremantle and then headed for Melbourne. Radio messages informed us that there was a wharf strike. The year was 1950, and strikes on the Australian coast were common. We were eventually nudged into our berth by a couple of tugs. Strikebound, we could be in port for weeks.

That evening, Sandy and I ventured ashore. We were aware that we could be called Pommy bastards by some of the Aussies we might meet. The main measure of intolerance was directed towards the ethnic groups from the Mediterranean region and middle European areas. Immigrants were coming in by the thousands.

Our first call was at an oyster bar. Sandy flirted with the girl who served us but all he got was a weary smile. We carried on and came to Flinders Street Station.

There was a pub just opposite called Young and Jacksons. We went in and that was the first time we saw *Chloe*. It was a magnificent painting, more than life-size, of a beautiful, totally naked young girl, painted by a Frenchman, Jules Lefebvre, I believe.

She epitomised the female form and over the years countless thousands of drinkers in the front bar had gazed at her. Once you had your first few glasses of ice-cold Australian beer, rubbed shoulders with the murmuring patrons and admired *Chloe*, it was your absolute duty to become a frequent visitor and devotee.

In those days, the pubs closed at six p.m. and from about five onwards there'd be drinkers six and seven deep making their last calls. It was probably the only period when admiration for *Chloe* was overtaken by the almost frenzied desire to sink a final schooner.

We finally got to Hong Kong and began our proper trading, up to Japan and down to Indonesia. Sandy and I were together on the *Tawi Tawi* on our first trip to Japan, still on our maiden voyage, when we were caught in a typhoon in Osaka harbour. We were alongside and the ship was pounded without mercy, six hours on one side, then the calm eye and then six hours from the other side. We were lifted up, pushed onto the wharf and through the sheds. We sank alongside the wharf, with only the bridge above water. Even shouted words an inch from the ear were swept away by the howl and shriek of the wind and spray.

Sandy came up to me, splashing calf-deep in the flooded chart room and punched me on the shoulder. He had a twinkle in his eye. He put his mouth to my ear and yelled, 'Marvellous…we're bloody invincible!'

We spent two months in a Kobe dockyard.

I think Sandy sensed that I needed guidance in matters regarding ladies. I was a novice. He led me like a lamb to slaughter and we spent the night in a house of ill repute. Sachiko was lovely and gentle. I was apprehensive, but the warm sake allayed my fears. Sandy, wise in his ways, cautioned me to let her be my guide. It turned out to be a wonderful, warm experience and I felt I was in love.

Sandy and I were together for years, ranging from Hong Kong, down to Tandjong Priok, Macassar in the Celebes and even flea-bitten Sariki up the Rejang river in Borneo. We even contemplated starting a poultry farm near Kuching in Sarawak. Another crazy plan of ours was to buy a coconut plantation, and even crazier to become patrol officers in Papua New Guinea. We'd let our imaginations run riot, dreaming of leading columns of police and porters into remote jungles where white men had never been.

There were typhoons. We went through a lot of them, hove to with props thrashing, riding them out in the Yellow Sea or south of Japan.

The *Tawi Tawi* came down to Australia several times and of course we made our pilgrimage to see *Chloe*. I think the last time I saw her was in '53.

Sandy and I were separated for about a year when I got transferred to the Formosa run. Finally when I came back to *Tawi Tawi*, he whisked me off to Repulse Bay to meet one of the company girls he'd fallen in love with. No more slumming for Sandy: he was now moving in sciety circles. It didn't last long. He was back with the rest of us, back to the kung fu, knocking back the beers and chatting up the tall Shanghai girls.

Finally, our contracts ran out. We flew home together in a Lockheed Constellation. He planned to spend time with his folks and then go to Southampton to get his mate's ticket. I stayed in Croydon with my parents and studied at Stockwell for my first class ticket.

I went to Bristol to stay with him and his parents. They ran a successful pub. His mum was a quiet, gentle woman and his dad was an older version of Sandy, jovial and boisterous.

We both got our certificates at about the same time. He was heading back to Hong Kong. Promoted to first officer, I decided to join the Greeks. They flew me to Houston, Texas, to join a tanker. I was on that vessel for more than five years solid, tramping the world.

Sandy and I kept in touch over the next few years. He was now a master and I wondered if he'd let his rank get to him. No, his letters arrived at intervals, always at Christmas, and then after about three years they stopped altogether. I speculated that as he was now about thirty-three he could have got married, perhaps was now a father with a host of things to do.

I reached the age of thirty-one. I was tired. I'd been at sea for more than a decade. I signed off in Philadelphia, was repatriated to London and then sailed out to Sydney.

It was now 1961. I arrived on a Friday and began work on the following Monday. I met a twenty-one-year-old brunette and we were engaged in three weeks and married in three months. I was a man in a hurry. We went up to Papua New Guinea for ten years and we raised a family there. I often wondered how many children Sandy had. I once wrote to the company but got no reply.

Time passed by. We left the tropics and settled in South Australia. I often wondered if, like me, Sandy had swallowed the anchor.

I reached sixty, then seventy, then seventy-five. The kids had grown up and were living their own lives. My wife and I were in our forty-fourth year together. We were comfortably off.

One day, being an artist, she said to me that she'd like to see the Dutch Masters exhibition being held at the National Gallery of Victoria. Why not, I thought. She made all the flight and hotel arrangements on the Internet, at which she was a whizz.

The exhibition was great and we had two enjoyable days down there. Suddenly, it hit me like a thunderbolt. My eyes picked up the signs of Flinders and Swanston streets and there, Young and Jacksons.

'My God, *Chloe's* in there.' I said excitedly, 'we've got to see her!'

We crossed the street and entered the pub. I expected to see her on the wall. I caught the barmaid's eye and asked where *Chloe* was.

'Upstairs,' she said, with a smile. 'She has her own bar now.'

We climbed the carpeted stairs, turned the corner and there she was: statuesque and magnificent. My wife was totally impressed. I'd often told her how Sandy and I had first seen her.

Here there was no beer-swilling mob. It was a quiet, discreet bar. The patrons were in their mid-fifties and beyond. We sat a central table so that we could gaze at her: I ordered a glass of the house red and a Riesling for my wife.

I noticed a few couples coming into the bar and standing in front of the painting, pointing, smiling and talking animatedly. I sensed that the man would be recounting to his wife how and when he first saw *Chloe*, and like me was on a pilgrimage.

We finished our drinks and were about to leave. My wife went to powder her nose. I stood in front of *Chloe*, letting my mind drift. A couple came up beside me. The man was short and chunky, possibly in his forties: brown-eyed and bushy haired. His wife was a pleasant look-ing woman, smiling as he spoke to her.

'Brings back memories, does it?' I said.

'Oh yes,' the man replied. 'The last time I saw her was in '81. I came here with my old man. He was always raving about her. He first saw her way back in 1950. When he heard that we were coming into the city he said, "Don't forget *Chloe*."'

I was nodding. 'Exactly. Nineteen-fifty is when I first saw her. In-credible.' I paused. 'Your old man…what was he doing in 1950?'

'He sailed out here from the UK. The ship was on its maiden voy-age.'

I must have gone a bit pale. My wife came up to me at that moment. I put my arm around her waist. I was shaking my head slowly.

'Your dad…is he Sandy Wilson?'

'My God,' the man said. Impulsively, he reached for my hand to shake it. 'You know him?'

'Sandy and I had our first cold beers here, looking at *Chloe*. She was downstairs then. How is he…is he…?'

'He's fine, coming up to eighty…still going strong. He came out here in '81, when Mum died. That's when we came here to see her. How long are you here for?'

'We fly back tomorrow morning,' my wife said.

'No time to waste then. He lives just ten minutes away. We'll take you there.' He laughed. 'Here we are, we've made a discovery and don't know each other's names.'

Introductions were quickly made.

Greg and Sandra drove us into suburbia, down a tree-lined street and up to a neat red-brick house. The four of us came up to the door.

Greg knocked and called out, 'Dad?'

We heard an answering voice. Greg placed his hand at the small of my back and brought me forward. The door opened and I was looking at a little old man with bushy grey hair, grey eyebrows and brown eyes peering from under them.

I felt the prickle of tears behind my eyelids. In a sort of husky whisper, I said, 'Sandy?'

His mouth opened and closed but no sound came.

Tawi Tawi…Chloe.

'God,' he whispered. 'Dickie.'

It seemed that everyone was weeping. Sandy and I were in a bear hug, patting each other's backs. I could feel his body shuddering.

It was a memorable day. We're keeping in touch.

The Cobra

He felt as though he had at last arrived in port. The final port. At anchor. Sitting on a slatted bench near Manly wharf watching the locals try their luck with the flathead and bream. There were hoots and shouts. The ferries coming in, blue water and red-roofed houses, and ships going through the Heads, as he had done so many times, looking shoreward and knowing that one day he'd be back. Australia in the 1960s was a brave new land with a future. The girls were tall and tanned, wearing bright summer dresses, and he'd carried the picture of them in his mind as they moved up and down George Street, right down to Circular Quay.

He had walked off the ship on Friday and found work on Monday. He had taken lodgings in Manly. At thirty, he had never driven a car, but after joining a driving school he had passed his test in five lessons. He was ashore after more than a decade at sea. He didn't even know how to use a coin-operated phone or handle a bank account. There was a lot to learn.

Still, he was content. The sun was comfortable and he felt drowsy, locked in an introspective shell, barely aware of the ferries coming and going, and the crowds of people. He was not yet a part of them. He was a stranger, or distant relative looking for a family to fit into. He'd been wandering too long, searching for a home. The words of a poem came to him. How did it go? '…the restless thrill of changing skies. Only for him who knows the ceaseless urge to go, go ever on, carried by the tide and trade winds pulsing surge, lured by the bright mirage of far off places, forests and jungles and bleak, frozen spaces…'

There was a nice young girl up at Quinton Road, living in the flat below him, with girlfriends. He had looked down from his window, seeing her in a swimsuit, sunbathing on a beach towel under the magnolia tree. They seemed to worship the sun. She was a little brunette with good legs. He'd gone down, somehow drawn there. For all he knew, she probably had a boyfriend, many of them, because there'd been a party the other night and he'd heard the laughter and music. It seemed it was their way of life, with football in the afternoon and Saturday-night beer parties and a lot of noise. It had been his first attempt to be friendly with the natives and he didn't mean that in a derogatory sense, a Pom communing with Colonials.

The girl had laid her book aside when he wished her good morning. He saw the name Durrell and it had something to do with animals. He commented that they must have had a good party. She came up on her elbows, looked at him and then said something about did he mean that they were too noisy, and that most people had a party on Saturday nights.

There was nothing he could say. He wasn't good at repartee. He'd never had the practice. One thing about them, they were rather forthright. She was only tiny. Pretty. How did one get to know girls, good girls? There must be a sort of social sequence, maybe drinks in a bar, beach parties, seeing a movie, meeting Mum and Dad and a tribe of aunts and uncles. He just looked at her, and she at him. It must have appeared that he was looking at her figure, because she drew the towel over her legs. It wasn't true. He'd muffed it. He murmured a soft goodbye as a sort of apology and moved away.

The girl watched him as he went to the backyard gate and fumbled with the latch, trying to get out. He seemed rather awkward. Not too bad-looking, she thought. He was certainly different.

That was last week, he reflected as he eased himself on the bench, but she kept cropping up in his mind and he'd try to keep her there but no, there were too many things jostling for position. A series of images came unbidden: Chile just a few months ago, then up through Panama, and signing off in Philadelphia, then down to Florida. The pictures came fast, of the Everglades and airboat rides, fishing for tarpon. Good things come to an end. Then up to New York, across the Atlantic to London, and out to Sydney. He seemed to be out of his body, looking down on himself, a lone figure on a bench. It wasn't long ago he was a young lad on the Indian plains, a schoolboy up in the Himalayas, sure-footed as a mountain goat. Only a dogwatch ago, he was on the wing of a bridge. Where was the young man who went deep sea so many years ago? He sat quietly while the sun began its descent and the first chill of evening came on. He was barely aware of the increased activity on the wharf as people returned, hurrying from the city.

The girl saw him as she turned on to the footpath. He was the only person not moving, almost unseeing as people went back and forth in front of him. She stepped off the path and paused to watch him. Something in his pensive gaze out to sea plucked a string in her heart. She had frequently thought of him standing tongue-tied, rebuffed that day he'd spoken to her. There was something different about him. He seemed vulnerable. Very unlike the brash, assertive young males she'd met, who'd never even opened a car door for her. She didn't believe he would be at all like them, she thought, as she approached.

He became aware of a pair of shoes, nylons and the hem of a blue skirt at the edge of his vision. He blinked and looked up at her.

'Hello,' she said. Her eyes were blue-green in a soft, oval face.

She had a white mohair jumper on, which he noticed she filled nicely. That kind of material left hairs on blue uniforms. The sight made no impact on him. He was in neutral gear, holding back thoughts that could be too presumptuous.

She sat beside him. 'You seemed to be far away.'

'Yes, I was,' he said, 'remembering things. It's nice here.'

'Do you come here often?' She asked.

'It's the first time really.' He looked at her and smiled. 'I have a day off, so I thought I'd see how the fishing is. How to bait a hook, how to cast a line, and learn from the real experts.'

'And did you?'

'Yes, but no one ever lets a fish go. They're just hauled up and left to gasp their lives away. In England, in the ponds and lakes, a fish is caught, handled gently, admired and released.'

She looked at him, intrigued. It was something she'd never heard of. Such a caring tradition. She hated cruelty to animals. It was probably why she liked Durrell's books so much.

'I've just bought a rod,' he continued, 'but I don't think I'll be using it much.'

'We thought you were an American. That slight accent, and you have a large car. We even thought you could be a rich American,' she smiled.

'Sorry,' he apologised. 'Must be because I was on the American run for five years, at sea. No, I was born in India.'

'More surprises,' she laughed. 'I've always been fascinated by those places, India, China. India, millions of people, heat, snakes and things that crawl. I suppose you've seen snake-charmers and cobras.' She pronounced it like cob, as in bob or corn on the cob.

He corrected her quietly. 'Not cob. It should rhyme with cove. Like cove-ra. Cobra. Yes, I've seen them. One struck at me once.'

She looked at him closely, taking in the steady blue eyes, somewhat faded, and the tanned face. A quiet, reserved expression. Yes, she believed it.

'How? How did it happen?'

'Well, it's a long story.' He paused. 'And it's getting cool. Would you like to go for a drive? Could you show me the way to Long Reef?'

'It's just up the road. That would be nice, as long as I'm home by six.'

They walked up the Corso and into Darley Road, to where his car was parked. His very first car, a Holden.

'Sorry about the fishing rod,' he said.

It was in the middle of the front bench seat, pointing down to the floorboards and up over the seat, almost touching the roof. She thought it was funny.

It was beautiful at Long Reef, looking down on the sea just as the sun began to set. Far out, a tanker was heading south. He talked all about the sea and the things he knew.

She listened intently, her body turned towards him. Suddenly she shook her head.

He paused. 'Perhaps I'm talking too much. I haven't talked so much for a long time.' He looked into her face, with its soft shadows.

'I'm listening,' she said, 'but you're going too fast. I don't want to miss anything. Tell me about the cobra.'

'Well, it's not much,' he said. He'd really begun to like this girl. He felt good about her. He wanted to tell her things. Wanted her to be a friend. He could sense that she liked him. Nineteen maybe, lovely face, bright questioning eyes. Petite. She, he and the car formed a threesome. It just seemed natural, despite their age difference. He smiled to himself.

'Why are you smiling?' she asked, smiling at him in turn.

'Happy, I guess.' He cleared his throat. Serious. 'Well, this cobra,' and he began to laugh.

'Now what,' she said.

He shook his head. 'Here we are. A thousand things to say. This scene in front of us. That tanker out there. Snakes, how did we get onto snakes? On that bench today, I was thinking how it all works out, how paths are set for us to follow. I'm a stranger here, haven't lived ashore for eleven years, still thinking of port and starboard and yet, here we are.'

She wanted to reach out and touch his face, so that her fingertips could feel his emotion. Instead, she narrowed her eyes in mock impatience. 'Are you going to tell me about this snake or not?'

'Well, this was in northern India, north-east of Delhi, a small place called Saharanpur. I was about sixteen at the time. We were having lunch and heard a commotion outside. Indians are quite excitable. A mob of them were on the veranda, all talking at once. Evidently, a cobra had been disturbed in a field by a cowherd and his cattle. The cattle had stampeded, causing the cobra to cross the road, chased by a crowd hurling stones and clods of earth. It had entered an orchard and gone into a small hut in which the watchman or chowkidar lived. He was still in there, trapped, hanging onto the bars of the window and screaming his head off. It was huge they said, and could we help? "Better take the gun and look," my dad said.

'I picked up the old Midland 12-gauge, with its long barrel and a couple of number eight cartridges, small shot. Not a gun for close work. I could hear the fellow shrieking from a long way off. The people outside were hurling stones and let off a cheer as I came up. The door was of the type that swung inwards, and the snake was behind it. There was no other way but to go in. I fed the cartridges in, shut the gun and eased back the hammers. I flattened myself against the door jamb and quietly entered the doorway, knowing the cobra had sensed, heard and smelt me come in.

'The crowd was silent now, holding its breath, I guess. I know I was. I took a step in. The door was still between us. I leaned to one side and looked at the snake. It was ready, and as I moved one step further, there it was, vicious and ugly, poised to strike, a quarter of its length raised, slanted upwards from the coiled base with the head half a metre off the ground. It was all of two metres long and there was just on half that distance between us.

'I knew the shot would come out like a solid ball. I froze. The snake spread its hood and arched its back in a sort of sinuous motion. It swayed back and forth, beady eyes glaring, decreasing and increasing its height and making a puffing sound. I felt cold all over. I thought to myself that if it struck, even with my finger on the trigger I wouldn't have time to pull. I stayed absolutely still, fascinated by the thin forked tongue speeding in and out of its lips. I had to get out of striking range and to where I could fire without hitting the man or the people outside.

'The snake seemed to cool down a bit and slowly lowered itself and then bumped its nostrils against a crack in the door, scenting the outside air. I took one big stride away and in a flash it struck at the last movement of my shoes. I felt it slam against the side of my heel in a sort of deflected strike that sent its head against the cement. You should have seen it then. Talk about angry! It reared back, spread its hood and the coils made a quick muscular adjustment and he rose up, making hissing sounds.

'My heart was racing. The crowd outside had seen the strike and let go a yell. Don't ask me how, but somehow I'd moved across the room, far enough now to fire. Very slowly, I brought the gun up. The cobra increased its height as if planning a long strike. I froze for about fifteen seconds and then brought the gun up to my shoulder, and, as I thought, it came up, gradually lifting higher following the muzzle.

'Then I had him front on. I lined up on the throat at the base of the hood and pulled the trigger. Deafening, a terrible kick! There was noise, shouting, pulverised cement trickling from a hole in the wall, and the writhing snake with its head against the wall just like a bloodied, black glove.' He stopped. 'Well, that's the story.'

She looked at him, her eyes scanning his face, as though searching for the boy of his past. 'What a different life you've had.'

She could see it all in her mind, transported there and looking into a cube that was a room, a figure, a gun, a shining black snake, a bang in her ears. She felt tears well into her eyes and she couldn't understand why, except that she didn't mind. She always was too emotional. Poor thing, she thought. Deadly, but the way it had been described, so brave and fearless. She could imagine it saying to him, stand back, no closer or I'll strike you, I'm warning you. She blinked and gave an embarrassed laugh. She dug for a tissue in her handbag.

'I'm sorry,' he said. In telling the story, he could feel himself reliving it, his senses alert and tingling. He reached out and touched her arm. 'Sorry,' he repeated.

She looked at him, as if searching for his inner feelings. 'I just felt so sorry.' There was a sheen in her eyes.

He nodded. 'I feel sorry too. What right had I to blow its head off? A thing like that, perfect, in its prime. It wasn't its fault. It was provoked. Oh, they were patting me on the back, I was a brave young sahib and all that, but I don't know. They took it outside, chucked it around, jumped on it, yelling and laughing. It's terrible in India, all over the Far East, senseless cruelty to animals.'

'I can imagine you there. I'd love to go. It would be fascinating.'

'For a girl, alone, it could be hard. Let me know and I'll come with you,' he smiled.

'D'you still want to travel? It's not out of your system, is it?'

'I've done enough for the moment. I'm home to roost. Apart from the time as a boy in India, I've never lived ashore. I don't know how. I'm still finding it strange.'

'Well,' her hand touched his briefly, 'if you need any help, you can call me.'

'Perhaps I will. Would you like to go for a drive some other time? Out in the country. I want to try billy tea with a gum leaf in it.'

'I'd love to.' She smiled at him. 'Just one thing: next time, could you put the fishing rod somewhere else?

The Pheasant

Tuesday brought a change in the weather. Sunshine poured down onto the city, old and new, astride the Salzach river, onto the drooping Linden trees and lush, saturated verdure of the Salzburg plain.

I looked through the window and saw my old pheasant friend taking slow, stately strides through the tall grass of the grounds of the St Rupert hotel. Like a proud galleon ploughing through a green sea, he was doing his rounds, pausing momentarily to adopt a stance, raise himself up, furiously flap his wings and emit a sharp, raucous cry, calling for a mate and proclaiming his territory. He was a ringneck and I called him Cedric, in memory of a pheasant I once had, just like him.

The weeks I'd spent here were punctuated by his regular, sharp cries, accompanied sometimes by the muted, distant pealing of the church bells at Herrnau. During my morning walks, I'd taken to feeding him with a pocketful of grain. I felt I had a bond with him, and I think Susan was aware of it. She'd been my secretary in Sydney for years and I felt that she knew me, enough to credit me with some sensitive feelings, enough to be a friend to a pheasant. It was part of a gentle probing, circuitous, feather-light testing between us that had been going on for quite a while. When she phoned from London to say she was coming, I arranged a room for her at the St Rupert.

I'd come here to put the finishing touches to my book and was staying with the Countess Ledohowska in her chateau on Hellbrunner Allee. I'd stayed with her before and she was a good friend. I felt flattered to be trusted with the great ring of keys that opened and shut the massive wrought-iron gates. I was also privileged to be able to descend to the dank cellar, with walls two metres thick, to change the fuses when the power failed. She had an impressive collection of wines down there.

The countess was an aristocrat of the old school and had her own chapel. Having Susan stay with me was simply out of the question. Besides, I was sixty and she a mere twenty-nine.

It was too good a day to be walking through the flat city streets, market squares, even though the rushing Salzarch river was a lovely frothing torrent bordering the main embankment. It was Susan's suggestion that we go for altitude and the sun-dappled ring of mountains. We took the 55 from Kleingmain to St Leonard Tal station, and then in the cable car to the top of Untersberg. It was a splendid panoramic view.

Thin, wispy shrouds of mist drifted by silently, teasing the view away from us, momentarily revealing fresh, snow-covered peaks in Bavaria in one quadrant, closing it off and opening up the vista of the Salzburg plain in the other. Black mountain choughs with yellow beaks and red legs floated in with the mist, landing close by when a gift of bread was a possibility.

A distant cross on a higher summit beckoned us.

'Shall we try?' she queried, looking at me in that direct, honest way. She was aware of the problem I'd had with my heart.

A quick image of her sitting on the edge of the bed in the cardiac unit came to me. Four years ago.

'Why not?' I said and we started.

First the descent and then the steady climb with the warm sun on our backs. The terrain was made up of broken flint, quartz and shale, very loosely packed and unstable.

Perhaps it was the almost metallic rattle and click-clack of sliding stones, and the defiles through which we trudged that stirred my imagination, or perhaps it was her mop of curly blonde hair, which reminded me of the actress Ingrid Bergman and flashed a particular scene through my mind from the classic movie *For Whom the Bell Tolls*. I paused and asked her if she'd seen it. She hadn't, not surprisingly as it was before her time. I was too out of breath to begin a description. She smiled and I put my arm around her. As a schoolbo, I'd had a crush on Bergman.

We finally reached the cross. I looked around and it seemed as if we were on the very top of Europe. Mountains in a rolling mass, some streaked with snow, all around, and down below lay the Salzburg plain, exposing its beautiful patterns of light and dark greens. The serenity of the summit was marred only by the penetrating, whining voice of an American lady urging her recalcitrant teenage daughter to hurry up. The girl, sullen and pinch-faced, sat huddled below a cluster of rocks, taking a succession of photographs.

We started down, back to the cable car station, glad of the descent, which however still taxed the calf and thigh muscles. Further down, we came upon a couple of Germans, talking rapidly and with animated gestures. One, with binoculars, was focusing down into a deep chasm and there on a small rocky outcrop was a small brown speck.

'*Was ist das?*' I asked.

'*Gams,*' the man replied.

'*Was ist gams?*'

The man shrugged. '*Gams ist gams,*' he laughed.

Fair enough, I thought. It was a mountain deer or goat.

'Good eating, I should think,' Susan said.

'Yes,' he asserted, 'the best!'

We reached the Bergbanhhof and while waiting for the cable car we sat at a slatted table and bench, out in the cold, fresh air. She had a Stiegl beer and I had an Obstler schnapps in a small, chilled glass. She looked radiantly healthy, with a flush over her features. I looked at her with affection. Over the past week, she'd become my companion. She'd checked through the manuscript with a practised eye and had given it her approval.

'Are you going to stay much longer?' she said.

'Perhaps a week, maybe, then a day or two in London.'

'Well, the book's finished and well before the deadline,' she smiled. 'My plane leaves from Vienna the day after tomorrow. I'm getting off at Bangkok and plan to relax on Koh Samui.' She paused and her fingertips touched mine. 'Why don't you meet me there?'

I nodded. 'A gem of an island, I believe.'

We caught the next cable car down, again marvelling at the view.

My eyes swept the German with the binoculars who was sitting in front of me. I tapped his shoulder and pointed. *'Gams.'*

He swung his binoculars up and a few seconds later smiled over his shoulder. *'Ja,* very good. Good for eating,' he repeated.

'Tough and gamey,' Susan whispered in my ear.

I'd always used the countess as a sounding board and later that evening I told her about it.

'Not *gams,*' she said. 'That is dialect. *Gems, gemsen* is the word. It has small horns.'

'A chamoix,' I probed.

'That is it, same thing,' she smiled.

Two days later, I said goodbye to Susan at the local airport for her short trip to Vienna.

She breathed perfume over me and kissed me on the cheek. 'See you,' she said.

'See you,' I nodded.

The next morning, I walked across to the St Rupert but couldn't find Cedric. The countess waved to me as I passed and continued waging her war of poisoned pellets against the moles in her lawn.

At the St Rupert, I talked to the man in charge and asked him about the pheasant.

'Ah,' he remembered, *'Ja,* Fraulein Susan, she had him for dinner.'

I walked back slowly, deeply saddened. A noble bird. On a plate. I felt like weeping.

In the distance I heard the Herrnau bells chiming softly.

Koh Samui had lost its appeal. Completely.

Typhoon

His name was Laidlaw. Some called him Ladybird, but only behind his back. I was young enough and sufficiently in awe of him to give him plenty of respect. After all, he had the DSO and bar, and the *Croix de Guerre*. I wish now that I had got to know him better, but at the time he joined the *Taitung*, as chief mate, I was a very young radio officer, earnest and honest enough, but without a serious thought in my head. Certainly not serious enough to warrant a study of the man and to try and fathom his torment – because tormented, as I discovered, he was.

We made a nice run up from Sydney and nosed into Taikoo dockyard in Hong Kong for our annual survey.

The marine super, over rum and coffee, told us we were getting an exceptional chief officer, adding in a cautionary way. 'Don't be fooled by appearances.'

He'd been a master in the Egyptian line for eleven years but had got out before Nasser nationalised it and fired its English officers. During the war, he'd been a commander in minesweepers in the Royal Navy and had been decorated for the dangerous work he'd done in the home ports and the Channel. He had later been seconded to the French and they had honoured him for his efforts in the maritime regions of North Africa. He'd been through a lot.

Time passed, and during subsequent voyages I got to know him better. It wasn't easy. He kept to himself. I can recall him, once, reminiscing about the war. The memory of it must have been horrible because his voice got softer, he closed his eyes and leaned back in the settee, raised his arm and laid the back of his hand on his forehead: the way a lady would simulate a faint.

He talked of Senegalese troops storming a German fortification, which had been softened up by heavy pounding from warships offshore. The Germans surrendered and came out, hands aloft, so many of them young, blond lads, who'd put up a good fight. They were made to kneel in the sand, faced by their Senegalese captors. The soldiers made their request, the French officers nodded and the slaughter began. Africans sitting astride young Aryans, fists clenched in their hair, arching their necks back and cutting their throats. He had turned away, unable to bear the sight, but the cries and screams would be with him forever. Then the seagulls came to peck.

We were on the Australia to Japan run, carrying cargo and about fifty passengers. Once we passed into the Barrier Reef, cleared Thursday Island and came into the Timor Sea, we'd change into our number ten uniforms, white jackets and trousers, generally looking quite resplendent. Particularly Laidlaw. He was a big man, heavy-shouldered, with strong thigh and leg muscles fully occupying the tailored trousers. I think it was the firm mouth, and steady unblinking gaze of his brown eyes, flecked with slivers of gold, that drew people's attention, before they glanced away, unable to reconcile the mincing gait, the swing of arms with wrists held out, and a handkerchief protruding from the cuff of his jacket.

He was a descendant of some noble Norman family. When young, he had a nanny. I had a fertile imagination and could picture someone like him, in days of yore, dressed in armour, mace in hand, trudging knee-deep in a bow-legged gait through bodies, laying about him in some fog-shrouded battlefield, slow and relentless with steady eyes glaring through his visor.

He was an exemplary officer, inspiring confidence. A perfect gentleman, very British and cultured, and on social evenings he always had a number of lady passengers around him.

A pattern began to emerge. On the Australian coast, he'd be absolutely sober and with impeccable behaviour, but when in Hong Kong he'd go astray, completely disregarding the ship and his duties. He was to be found in the Peninsular or Hong Kong hotel on a monumental binge, sitting quite alone, erect in his chair with a steady gaze, imperious in fact. The second mate and I made the mistake, once, of going up to him, just to be affable. He held us captive for five hours, buying Scotches, saying barely more than a score of words, just sitting upright, eyes bloodshot, a stubble on his chin, but apart from a rumpled suit there was little to show that he'd been on a two-day ingestion of alcohol. It was a nightmare.

The planned delights of Hong Kong and the Kung Fu bar down Des Voeux Road had to be postponed. Then inexplicably he got up and walked steadily out into the night. He came back to the ship the next day, slept for twelve hours and emerged on deck looking clear-eyed and immaculate in his white uniform. No one said a word, not even the captain. We could only conjecture that it was some immense problem he had to deal with, or possibly forget. His three- or four-day lapses were more than compensated for by his three- or four-month periods of complete abstinence and dedication to duty.

In Sydney, he had friends, but we never quite knew who they were. He dressed rather well, generally in flannels and tweeds, and the people we sometimes saw him with were certainly well off. The women were elegant. They could have been from the British High Commission. They talked that way. While we slummed it, crawling from pub to pub, starting at Circular Quay, and up George Street, he no doubt dined well. Let's just say we had different lifestyles and were content to go our separate ways, or were we? If the truth be known, I think there were some of us who rather envied him his flair.

On one trip to Japan, we had among our passengers a young country girl, daughter of a wealthy grazier. She was a lovely girl, about twenty-two years of age, the same as me, and we got on well. I forget her name. She had very blue eyes, freckles, good regular features and a bubbly personality. A nice figure too.

During social evenings when there was horse racing, bingo and movies, I noticed that Laidlaw was beginning to monopolise her, without being too obvious. Nothing much happened, and I didn't expect anything because after all he was almost twenty years her senior. I mean, I never saw them on deck after dark, hanging around the lifeboats.

Nothing much happened with me either, except for the odd kiss and cuddle. Just a good voyage, nice enough evidently because on subsequent berthings in Sydney, she came down to renew acquaintances. I liked her a lot, but I was in no mood for heavy romance, content to just muck around as usual. I wish now that I'd taken the chance and gone bush with her to see the property, learn to ride a horse and chase a kangaroo or something. Laidlaw on the other hand took the opportunity, and at the end of one trip stayed at her homestead for a few days.

I missed a chance to get to know him better on one of the northern legs of the trip, when we came to Hong Kong. He asked me if I'd ever been to an investiture. When I said no, he asked if I'd be interested in seeing one, as he was getting a bar to one of his medals, to be pinned on by the governor. Full parade and what not. It meant getting dressed up like a pox doctor's clerk, mixing with the hoity toity, tea and tab nabs and cocking the little finger, so I made some feeble excuse. In fact, it wasn't all that feeble because the second mate and I were going to meet two ladies, wives of naval officers, whom we'd come to know. But that's another story.

Had I got to know him better by going to that investiture, by talking to him, becoming more friendly, would it have altered the final outcome? I think he was wanting to talk. Would I have been able to fathom the man, reach into his past and understand why he did what he did. If, in fact, he did what they say he did. It's still a mystery. But how can you put a wise head on young shoulders?

A few months later, on the northern leg and due to arrive in Osaka in twenty-four hours, I picked up the first report of a typhoon named Ruby, issued by Tokyo Kemigawa Observatory. Its position was fixed as a hundred miles north of Iwo Jima, moving north-west and intensifying. I took the report to the captain in the wheelhouse.

He put on his glasses and pulled out a chart. He marked the position and looked fixedly at it for a long time, moving his false teeth in and out. Finally, he nodded. 'Keep an eye on it. I hope we're out of Osaka before it hits.'

Reports from Guam, Hong Kong and Zikawei Observatory in Shanghai conflicted as to the exact location, but agreed that the velocity was in the region of a hundred knots. Guam's observation seemed to be most reliable since it was prefixed, 'Air reconnaisance'.

We began to roll moderately that night, in a low, long swell of constant direction, an indication that a big disturbance was on the way. Eighteen hours later, Ruby was south of Okinawa, accelerating and showing signs of entering the Yellow Sea. The wind velocity was now a hundred and twenty knots. If it continued towards the China mainland, we'd be all right. But the typhoon continued to be unpredictable. She slowed down, curved tentatively, hesitated and then after twelve hours of procrastination, just after the *Taitung* had berthed In Osaka, she headed for the main island of Honshu. It played havoc along the Ryukyu Chain and came barrelling along, with Osaka and Kobe in the way.

At this time, the Korean War was on and all Japanese harbours were more or less under American control. The captain asked for a tug to take us off the wharf, so that we could head for the open sea and face the typhoon there. The harbour master was of the opinion that Ruby would move further east and hit Yokohama, and the tug was refused.

The sky was a dull, slate-grey colour and a steady drizzle swept down, placing a blanket of oppressive dampness and chill over the harbour. At dusk, the first real gusts began to arrive. Hatches were battened down. Extra ropes and wire hawsers were secured to the bollards on the wharf. Passengers were advised to stay below.

Kobe Radio reported that the centre would strike within twelve hours and, as if in immediate answer to the warning, all late-comers came labouring in, humping their engines, scores of small craft, coasters, barges and fishermen with smoke billowing flat from their funnels, rolling heavily as they came through the breakwater.

The *Taitung* began to move in response to the heavy swell sweeping in, bumping against the wharf despite the taut restraining ropes. The wind velocity increased, up and up, 100, 120, 150, full, lashing hurricane gusts. It reached maximum force in the early hours of the morning. The harbour was a boiling mass of white water and instead of the conventional waves, huge cascades and spouts were flung up and sent crashing down, or were carried away as continuous sheets of spray, reducing visibility to less than a metre.

Above all was the deafening screech of the wind, the whole fury of nature giving voice and defying man to describe it. The ship heaved and groaned, struggling against the immense strength of the wind and mighty heave of confused seas. In the bucking wheelhouse, everyone stared through spray-lashed windows at the fury outside, doing its will in the inky blackness. Mere mortals gathered together in the yellow light, protected by four flimsy bulkheads, imprisoned by the lashing hand of the wind and sea. The pressure was so great that the needle of the aneroid barometer was leaping jerkily, in movements spanning as much as two inches, behaving frantically, and the very bulkheads seemed to expand and contract like the sides of a flimsy biscuit tin.

Then we felt the fore and aft ropes snap and the ship began to pound against the wharf, a heavy thumping crunch along her entire length, being forced off by the force of compressed water, restrained by the two remaining wire ropes and then slammed back again, on and on every half a minute. It was impossible to see the damage, but the whole side of the ship was bound to look like a vast sheet of corrugated iron. It was up to the rivets holding the steel plates together, hammered in at John Brown's shipyard in Greenock, to do their job.

The maelstrom lasted six hours and then with startling suddenness we found we could talk to each other without shouting. The barometer needle stopped jumping crazily, the pressure on our eardrums eased and the shriek of the wind died to a low howl. Now there was a new sound, the cries of thousands of seabirds, gulls, petrel, gannets in dense flocks milling around as far as the eye could see. They landed on the masts, the bridge, crosstrees, on the hatches and even down into the passage-ways. Frightened and exhausted, driven by the typhoon across hundreds of miles of ocean and gradually drawn into the eye of the storm where they remained, effectively caged in the calm eye, carried along as if in an insulated cocoon.

The captain's first thought was for an assessment of damage, securing the ship in preparation for the next blast, and then for food. Laidlaw and others made a hull inspection, and as expected the hull was in a terrible mess. A dry dock job, for sure. The engine room reported some leaks, but nothing serious.

'We have an hour before we get hit again,' the captain muttered. 'I don't like the look of that Greek.'

She was a 10,000 tonner, the *Eugene Chandris*. She was uncomfortably close and had obviously dragged her anchors. Up on her bow her mate and crew were letting chain go, while her prop thrashed the water as she tried to go astern.

A steward arrived with coffee and sandwiches, followed by Laidlaw with the report that the hospital aft was completely wrecked, ventilators smashed and one lifeboat gone. All passengers were safe, though frightened.

Then the first gusts arrived from the opposite direction and within minutes the low howl of the wind began to rise to a higher note, and the familiar bucking started again. The birds faced into the wind, streamlining themselves, but were plucked away, one by one and sent hurtling on with their plaintive cries fading into the rushing noise of the wind. Whole flocks went past at incredible speed, blurred white puffs, as though fired from a cannon.

An oil storage deport and a small hamlet that had been protected in the lee of a hill during the first half now felt the full force coming from the opposite direction. In the rapidly dwindling visibility, the havoc could be seen as the village blew apart. Roofs were stripped, galvanised sheeting was ripped off and the sheets, like deadly scythes, cut through buildings and tall trees, decapitating them. The noise of the wind reached a crescendo, and before the milky shroud of flying spray and torrential rain cut visibility off completely, we saw entire clusters of full forty-four-gallon oil drums rising like bulky black birds, tumbling high, end over end, carried at a hundred and twenty knots like projectiles out of control.

We hung on as the *Taitung* started more frequent and severe crunches against the wharf. The waves began their cascading action, huge eruptions of water reaching as high as the crosstrees, and all on the bridge were mesmerised by the sight of a harbour tug struggling gamely for the lee shore, too late. An involuntary cry went out as the tug was hurled upwards so that its bottom cleared the wave tops by several metres. There it hung, seemingly suspended while its crew were plucked off, small toy shapes disappearing into the sea, before the plunging bow hit the waves and the whole vessel went under, engulfed. At least seven men died then.

There was a sudden shout of alarm. The huge bow of the *Eugene Chandris*, like a giant blade rising and falling, appeared darkly on the port beam. She had dragged her anchors again and was bearing down on us.

The captain bit his lip and his face crumpled for a fleeting moment. He crossed over to the engine room voice pipe and shouted down it. 'Prepare to abandon. Port beam, brace for ramming' He remained there, standing hunched over the brass tube, head down and breathing deeply, as though sorting himself out.

I looked over to Laidlaw. He was quite composed. From the time of the first gusts, adrenalin had been racing through me. I was seething with excitement. I was sure the *Taitung* was invincible. Nothing would happen to her.

Faint shouts and the clatter of winches came from the bow of the Greek vessel. Out of sight and, without doubt, her prop was thrashing the water in efforts to go astern. We briefly sighted small spray-lashed shapes, bent double, high on her bow moving jerkily as they manned the winches, fighting for their lives. A loose handhold and a slip meant death. She came on, metre by metre, plunging up and then down, down till water creamed over her bow rail, up until her red-leaded bottom and depth markings showed. Up and down, knifing forward until she was ten metres from the *Taitung*.

Fearfully envisaging being cut in half, we hung on and waited. I felt the first real clutch of fear. A fleeting image of immersion in frothing water, a mouth wide open, and no sound. The *Eugene Chandris* continued to bear down and then imperceptibly began to retreat, slowly backing away into the spray and rain till she was just a blur, and finally lost to sight at about fifty metres.

The wind screamed in a sudden burst of fury and there was a thunderous crash and rending, ripping sound above the wheelhouse as the roof of the bridge gave way. A jagged, gaping hole appeared, seeming to expand every second. In moments, we were ankle deep in water as rain poured in. The radar scanner, DF loop and aerial lead-in box had disappeared.

Simultaneously, a six-metre-high tidal wave slammed into the harbour, a gigantic wave rushing headlong. It picked up the *Taitung*, snapped the ropes and steel hawsers and took the ship onto the wharf, shoving all eight thousand tons of her sideways into a wharf shed. The entire structure collapsed, crushing a score of Japanese wharf labourers who were clinging to the girders inside.

The ship disengaged itself from the tangled wreckage and rolled back, grinding her hull on the wharf and fell back into the sea. There was absolute chaos. I can still remember the shrill sound of the engine room voice pipe piercing through the cacophony of the wind, spray, rain and of metal grinding against the wharf.

I saw the captain's face crumple and sobs came from his throat as he shouted down to the engine room, 'Abandon ship!'. Spittle hung from his lips and his Adam's apple jerked up and down.

We were holed and flooding down below, and he was losing his ship, and himself. Laidlaw seemed to sway, or rather glide towards him, lay a hand on his shoulder and lead him into the chartroom. It was a sorry sight to see the old man, shoulders hunched, head down, seated on the daybed, water pouring onto his shoulders and sloshing around his feet.

Laidlaw quietly took command. He ensured that everyone was out of the engine room. The third mate was despatched to check on the passengers. His assumption of command seemed miraculously to have some effect on the elements. Within minutes, there was a noticeable lessening of the fury outside. The slamming against the wharf ceased as we took on more water, and then we touched bottom. All the crew's quarters and the lower cabin deck were below water, leaving the upper deck, lifeboats and bridge above. We sat firmly in the ooze.

It was several hours before the turmoil in Osaka harbour eased and the land again came into view. There was destruction everywhere. Small townships, hamlets and harbour installations were in ruins. Tugs and small craft lay on their sides as much as four and five kilometres inland, and one of the first things we saw was a Japanese coaster of about three thousand tons going through the last few minutes of her struggle. She was listing to port at about fifty degrees, suffering the effects of the heavy swell, and still mountainous but subsiding seas. She listed more and more while her crew scrambled onto her steeply banked side, hanging on. With a final lurch, she rolled over with a heavy sigh, exposing the entire length of her red-leaded bottom, surrounded by the small bobbing heads of her crew, buoyed up with life jackets.

The next morning, the dead began to float up, grotesque, bloated figures, face down, bumping quietly, almost apologetically against the ship's side. Men, women and children, their dark hair fanning out like moving tendrils. The Chinese crew were unnerved, and using long poles they pushed the bodies onwards to drift with the tide.

The captain stayed in his cabin. Some said he was on the gin. Laidlaw was in command, here, there, everywhere. He considered it imperative for us to contact Hong Kong. With the help of the crew hurling lines, the aerial down-leads were recaptured and I raised GZO on Stonecutters Island. Laidlaw discussed matters at length in the captain's cabin and a host of long messages were sent to the company, describing events and giving damage reports.

In due course, we were pumped out and towed to Kawasaki dockyard, where we spent two months. Glorious, an unexpected holiday spent mainly in Nancy's Bar, just off the Motomachi. We then steamed for Taikoo dockyard in Hong Kong, and spent a further six weeks there.

Word filtered down from head office that Laidlaw was to be given command of the *Wusan*. She was nearing completion in Greenock and he'd fly back to bring her out. In the meantime, for us, it was back on the Australia–Japan run, back to the beaches, the glorious suntanned girls and cold beer at Young and Jacksons. A return to normal after all the excitement.

I signed off in Sydney a few months later and returned to the UK. I got the odd letter from the second mate and in one he said that Laidlaw had packed it in and had married the grazier's daughter. With his young wife, he now moved in the social circle, and their photographs were often seen in glossy magazines. A baby girl was born not long after the marriage but survived only a few months.

I went back to radio college and got a first class PMG certificate as a chief radio officer and then joined the Greeks. They flew me from London to Houston, Texas, to pick up a tanker. I got another letter from the second mate, forwarded to Tampico saying that Laidlaw had blown his brains out. I was shocked to read that.

To this day, I still can't understand it. Such a drastic, permanent thing. Perhaps he'd done everything, tried it all, seen everything and there was nothing green any more. He'd seen death and seen life. I wonder what he saw in that last instant, that moment of truth. Was it a woman's face or that of a child? Did he see heaving seas and blood spattered sand, and hear the distant sound of gunfire and the plaintive cries of seagulls? Whatever...I'm sure he sat erect, face firmly set, and that he had a steady hand.

Koh Samui

I had this feeling of dissatisfaction. It was a constantly returning thought which I was aware of as an insidious, probing and destructive element in what promised to be a blissful time. I was being irrational and was not prepared for criticism and close scrutiny.

I was going to Koh Samui to thrash out a novel, chew and masticate it and to find out why I was drying out, and what was wrong. I was in a mood, and my wife, sensing it, quietly bided her time.

The Dash 8 twin-engined turbo prop took us over the Gulf of Thailand, heading south. Koh Samui appeared as a green emerald, coconut-clad in an azure sea. I silently cursed the cowboy at the controls as we came in too fast in my estimation, down, down to palm tree top level, and dropped in with a thump.

We checked into the five-star Imperial, the ultimate in comfort. It fronted onto the sea by way of a landscaped pool, with sculptured rocks and palm trees, surrounded by multicoloured beach umbrellas, reclining chairs, bougainvillea and green poolside grass. Gorgeous bronze bodies lay around. Young honeymooners from Rome, Frankfurt and Stockholm. It was too good and made me angry.

That evening, I told my wife we were going to slum it. We walked down Chaweng beach to the Maeo restaurant. It was up on stilts with a thatched roof, barely ten metres from the hiss and suck of waves lapping up on the beach. Basic benches and trestle tables provided the decor for us and the other clients. While enjoying my second cold Singha, I tuned in to the conversation and absorbed the atmosphere. My wife was aware of my concentration as she sipped her lime and tonic water. There were a couple of tanned, strongly built Germans, bare-chested, playing chess in a haze of cigarette smoke. A New Zealander and two girls from Bristol, on their way to Australia. Their big adventure. Young and full of enthusiasm and courage.

The shark curry was very good. I was told it was caught that morning. With it I had plain boiled rice, unspoilt. The staple of life. All well worth thirty baht. My wife enjoyed her vegetarian mixture of sweet and sour.

Walking back along the beach, I chose the moonlit shadows cast by a clump of palm trees to relieve myself.

'How's that,' I said, 'froth on froth,' just as the last wave ran up the beach.

'Not bad,' she said. 'OK, looking ahead, what d'you see?'

A feeling of irritation stirred in me. I hated being tested. I'm not competitive.

'All right. Grey, humped rocks bathed in moonlight, rising from a black sea with waves leaving silver threads on the beach.'

'And what d'you hear?'

'The lap of waves, the hiss of sand at my feet.'

'How does it feel?'

'Soft and powdery, touched by the coolness of night.'

I had laboured to respond. It had taken perhaps fifteen seconds and I still felt the lingering touch of irritation. Prose. In the past, I'd been accused of too much verbosity in my prose. I began to work myself up. In novels, I was able to expand, explore, let my imagination run glorious riot, but I could hear the censure from my critics, my wife and daughter.

'Cut it down. Too much wordage. Too much flowery stuff.' I sweated over those paragraphs.

I switched to short stories. I could hear them. 'Make every sentence count. Make it succinct.' Words, descriptions had been my forte. I felt that I was now writing with one eye shut and one hand tied behind my back. I gave them my submissions.

'Not good enough. Cut it down.' I knew they were trying to help but they were cruelly blunt. and emasculating.

Now, here on Chaweng beach I was in the mood to defend myself.

I knew within myself that I hadn't lost the skill, but was acutely aware that it would take hard work to climb back to that glorious period when rich, expressive sentences flowed from my pen.

'I'm trying to help you,' she said, unaware of the time bomb within me, ready to explode. 'I'm going to give you exercises. Remember everything that's happened today. Pick on anything, something fleeting, right down to one second and describe what you saw.'

I ground my teeth. I was the writer. I saw the absolute sense of what she was proposing. It would make my brain work, but I resented it.

'I had it once,' I challenged. 'I used to write beautiful stuff but between the two of you you destroyed it. I went to the short story, cutting, cutting all the time, and what happened? I lost the lot.'

'The trouble is, you don't listen,' she said.

I flared up, enraged. It was a sentence I'd been hearing for decades. 'Here I am,' I shouted and put my fingers behind my ears, flaring them out like an elephant, 'listening.'

'I'm not going to say another thing.'

'Look,' I said, 'what you're saying has merit. I just don't like this catchphrase of yours, about not listening.'

'All right. I'll take that as an apology.' I'd never ever heard her say she was sorry. 'I'm glad you find what I'm saying has merit.'

I sighed. 'It has merit, but just remember that on a certain evening on Chaweng beach I did listen.'

'I think we should go back and have an early night.'

'I'll come in later. I'll go down to those lights and pick up some atmosphere. That's what I'm here for.'

I reached the Fair House restaurant, set back from the beach, an oasis of light. Beside it was a lonely, magnificent palm tree. I put my arm around it as I went in. It was full of Australians, young men and women, some Japanese and a Thai waiter, in shorts and a stained T-shirt. Too casual, cool and conversant with European ways.

I was thirsty and ordered a large Singha. I mulled over my situation and agreed to myself that my wife was right. She generally was.

I saw a young girl in jeans and sneakers. She smiled at the waiter who approached her and as he passed I ordered another beer. The girl was quite sweet. High cheekbones, narrow face and small delicate mouth. It irked me to see her smile at him. Was I being too critical, I wondered. I looked away to see an Australian pouring salt on his food, shake after shake. Poor bugger. Twenty years, or less, he'd realise his mistake.

I glanced at the girl and saw that she was watching me. I was tempted to smile, but one in her group wearing a blue singlet was looking at me. I signalled to the waiter and ordered another beer.

I felt the urge to jot things down and pulled out the small notebook I kept in my hip pocket. I felt that the economy of Koh Samui was geared mainly on the youthful, their romance and lust. They came from all over Europe to fornicate in hot hotel rooms with the scent of jasmine wafting through the slatted windows, or on the pristine beaches, stepping out of discos that catered to their needs, the Black Cat, Fiesta and Blue Moon, into the warm night air, lolling in the tepid sea. I resented them their youth. The thought of returning to my wife appealed to me. She would have showered and was probably reading one of her store of historical novels.

I called the waiter over and asked for the bill. A hundred and fifteen baht. I paid and he came back with the change in a leather folder. It didn't seem the right amount.

I gave you five hundred baht,' I said. I was quite sure.

'You gave me two hundred baht,' he replied.

We looked at each other. He wasn't at all servile.

I drew the money out of the folder, put it in my pocket and walked out. It was probably the first time in my life I'd not left a tip. My wife frequently said I was too generous. I walked into the pool of light bathing the sandy beach and had gone barely fifty metres when the first inklings of doubt entered my mind. Perhaps I had given him only two hundred baht. I was getting more assured of it as I tramped through the sand. I was appalled. If there was one thing, I was fair. I felt I'd demeaned myself. What were his feelings? What obscenity against Europeans did he mutter as he cleared the table? What seeds of anger had I sown and how could I make amends? It must have been the beer.

I had to do the decent thing. I went back to the restaurant to find that it was closing. The Australian group were coming down the wooden stairs and the girl smiled as she passed by me. I went in, saw another Thai and asked where the waiter was. He called out and the waiter came out of the kitchen. He approached, unsmiling and hostile.

'Here,' I said and handed him a fistful of baht. 'Sorry, my mistake.'

'No,' he said.

I reached out and took his hand. 'Shake hands. My mistake. Sorry.' I smiled. He nodded and took the money.

'All right?' I said.

'OK,' he replied and gave a small smile.

I walked back slowly to my luxurious, air-conditioned room. I told my wife what had happened. 'I was wrong and I made it right.'

'Good,' she said, turning a page. 'You've earned his respect. Hurry up, have a shower and come to bed.'

I turned towards the bathroom.

'Why don't you write about it?' she added.

The Fugitive

I think I have a friendly face which threatens no one. I say this because I'll pass total strangers in the street and they'll smile, or I'll sit in a train, make fleeting eye contact and get a responsive nod.

I feel good about it because it means my inner self must be at peace, most of the time. Besides, my wife, who knows me better than I know myself, can read my thoughts and deduce my emotional state by scanning my face with a quick glance, and it's been a long time since I've heard her say, 'Stop frowning.'

I had little to frown about one particular morning when she and I travelled up to London, where she had an appointment with a publisher. While she was closeted with the director, upstairs, I settled myself comfortably in a lounge chair in the receptionist's office to read a book.

It wasn't easy. The phone was a constant barrier to the thread of continuity.

The receptionist fielded each query efficiently, in beautifully articulated tones. 'Terribly sorry, Mr Hall is in conference. No, I'm afraid Mr Ziegler is out at the moment. Yes indeed, we do have that, I'll transfer you.' And then a change, 'Yes, darling, a Siamese, thoroughbred of course.'

After a hectic spate of incoming calls, she looked at me and rolled her eyes heavenwards. 'The system is so antiquated. I can't put anyone on hold.'

'Have you complained?' I said sympathetically.

'Indeed, but they're really not aware of the difficulties,' and she swept her eyes to the upper floor. 'Hopefully by Christmas,' she smiled.

'I take it you have a new pet?'

Her face lit up. 'A Siamese sealpoint kitten.'

'I have one,' I said. 'Actually, it's a question of who owns who.'

It appeared, after a fragmented discussion between incoming calls, that she was devoted to animals in general and believed she should have been a vet. The cruelty to animals in Spain, Egypt and other places in the Middle and Far East was unbearable, and animal welfare groups were recipients of her tithe.

She found time to make us a cup of tea, and I began to warm to her. She was in her late fifties and blessed with flawless skin. She was of that particular breed of Englishwomen who are dark-haired, brown-eyed and just slightly olive-skinned, as opposed to the blue-eyed, peaches and cream complexioned women, generally associated with English ladies of breeding. Perhaps this lady, Rene, could trace her lineage directly back to Norman times, with a possible touch of Seville. I let my imagination run.

'There was a time when I had six poodles,' she mused, and proceeded to name them. 'They all lived on our yacht in Monte Carlo. It was berthed just beside Onassis's *Christina*.'

'You knew him?' I said.

'Oh yes. I knew Aristotle well, and Christina,' she nodded and gave a half smile. 'Exciting times, parties, budding romances,' she said with a mischievous twinkle. 'Anyhow, as a matter of fact, I gave his son, he'd just turned fourteen, one of my poodles for his birthday. You should have seen the look on his face. A dear boy. Aristotle came over and wanted to know how much it cost. Imagine. I told him the look on the boy's face was payment enough.' She sighed. 'They were heady days.'

I wondered privately what had reduced her to her present mode of occupation, and she seemed to sense it.

'My husband was a Greek. Charalambos Pateras, Pampi for short. He opened a bank in Monte Carlo. Very succesful,' she paused, 'then came a crash and he absconded. A fugitive. I've never seen him since.'

'Sorry,' I muttered. 'It's a coincidence but I served on Greek ships for about five years, owned by N.G. Pateras.'

'Oh!' she blurted out, 'Pampi's brother. He was one of my beaus, an old flame.' Her face came alive. 'He'd always come to see me. I was on the stage, a Windmill girl. Oh, I've been in so many West End plays,' and she enumerated several. 'I've worked with them all, Sellers, Milligan, Redgrave,' she enthused.

'You ought to write a book,' I said.

She smiled. 'I've been asked to do that many times. I've been privy to many…' and she crinkled her eyes. 'I'd be sued. The things I could tell about the London scene!'

A few weeks later, my wife and I were at Stourport, about to embark on a canal boat for a week's trip to Nantwich, up the Staffs and Worcs canal, and then into the Shropshire Union. We were looking forward to it with enthusiasm, our imaginations fired by tales of ingenuity and fortitude of industrial barons of the nineteenth century who caused the canals, locks and aqueducts to be built.

We were shown to our cabin by a tall, pretty young woman, chief mate and girlfriend of our youthful captain. Two other girls formed the crew of the two boats, one powered by a diesel and the other, the butty, which was towed behind. Both vessels were beautifully appointed, immaculate and literally gleamed with varnish and polished brass.

We were introduced to two genteel ladies from Surrey, lifelong friends and now companions in widowhood. British to the core, and compendiums of knowledge, we were to discover, about flowers of the countryside and hedgerows of England, both partial to a little after dinner sherry, and Scrabble fiends to boot.

My wife, in her fashion, went to explore and discovered the one other passenger, in the butty. When I followed her, she said, 'Meet Frank.'

I shook hands with an old man, who, and I'm hesitant but I must say it, looked like a frog. His touch was clammy. He was seated and his walnut eyes peered up at me from under heavy, hooded eyelids. His skull was hairless and blotched, his ears were plastered close to his head and his cheeks were fleshy, folded layers which drooped in loose jowls off the sides of his face, framing a jutting mouth with a protruding lower lip. The overall impression was of a large head on narrow shoulders, a sunken chest and a huge belly resting on his knees. His hands, covered with large liver spots and freckles, lay on his ample paunch.

'Frank's an American. He's been onboard for months,' she added.

'I like it,' he said flatly, his face betraying no expression.

I had the feeling he'd assessed me, as I had him, and hoped his astute eyes had not deduced the image I'd created, which, I must hasten to add, was tempered by some sympathy. I could read nothing in his gaze, except perhaps an imagined resentment over the invasion of his privacy. Frankly, I was glad he was onboard. Travel to me means people, rather than places, and I've always had an affinity towards Americans based on personal experience.

At dinner that evening, we all met formally for the first time, and like all people who travel, we explored the world with the assistance of personal anecdotes.

Frank masticated his food thoroughly, and regrettably allowed the pulp, in the form of a thin froth, to coat his lower lip before his darting tongue drew it in.

I mentioned we were planning a trip to Austria, Poland, Berlin and so on.

He nodded. 'Don't like Austria. Used to. Too many tourists. Had a chalet outside Salzburg, place called Werfenweng. Know it?'

'Pretty place. We did some walking there once.'

'Been to Switzerland?' he asked.

'Years ago.'

'I have a house there. I stay a few months every year or so, near Neuchatel.' He continued chewing. 'Been to West Virginia?' he said.

'No.'

'It's where I live. Finest country,' he asserted.

As dinner continued, it appeared that Frank owned houses all over the globe. I gave him the honours and admitted that my travel was limited to visiting ports, as opposed to long sojourns inland, except for the odd tourist trip.

'I was with the Greeks for many years,' I explained, 'just tramping. South America, Chile, Argentina, that area.'

'What company?' he asked.

'N.G. Pateras, out of New York.'

His eyes gave a flicker and he stopped chewing. 'I know the name.'

'It's strange,' I said, sitting back, 'but just the other day I was talking to a lady in London, and when I mentioned the Pateras name in connection with being at sea, she exclaimed at the coincidence because N.G. was an old flame of hers. She had married his brother. Interesting lady, lived in Monte Carlo for years…'

Frank wiped his mouth with a napkin and awkwardly eased himself away from the table. Not a word was spoken. Dessert was yet to come. We all exchanged glances.

'Did we say something wrong?' one of the old ladies ventured.

'Well, I was doing most of the talking,' I said and made a mental check, but absolved myself of guilt.

The girl crew serving dinner appeared to take it in their stride. 'With Frank, that's quite normal,' they said. After dinner, when the skipper dropped in to discuss the next day's plans, he also confirmed that the old fellow could be unpredictable and quite rude.

On the following morning, Frank failed to appear at breakfast. A quick check showed that his cabin was empty and his single suitcase was gone. Our nine a.m. departure was delayed while the skipper and crew scoured the basin, then Stourport itself, checking the bus and railway stations, the taxi company, and then finally advised the police.

We finally left the basin, went through a couple of locks and entered the canal, and with it came the pleasure of watching the English countryside go by. A very enjoyable experience.

After a few days, Frank became a distant memory. A week later, at Nantwich, we said goodbye to our friends.

'Any news of Frank?' we asked when the skipper came back from phoning his head office.

'None at all. He's done a bunk.'

I wonder if his real name was Pampi Pateras, the fugitive.

The Wandering Albatross

It was cold and wet, with grey scudding clouds and slanting rain-gloomy weather. I'd made no conscious thought to plumb the 'Deep Well' but unbidden thoughts came up of a man I'd never met but nevertheless regarded as a friend: like looking at a blurred photograph.

He was my mentor, who read my inner thoughts, and mingled in the blur I saw a picture of myself, younger, looking lost and alone. Also there were ships. I saw slate-grey heaving seas and plunging bows in the winter North Atlantic, sparkling sun dancing on the warm Humboldt stream off Peru and Chile, the jungle on the banks of the Panama Canal and the frothing turbulence of storm-tossed waves coming up to Cape Hatteras.

The picture was there in the blink of an eye and then gone. All that I'd seen in that instant was true and no figment of my imagination. I'd been there. I'd done things. I'd been moulded by events and here and now I was the product of all that had happened then, before then, and since. I could almost hear my mentor asking me to tell him about it.

I'd spent eleven years at sea sailing all over the world, searching for myself. Like many others in this changing world, I'd been part of an exodus from a former colony to the mother country, out of place and insecure. The last five years had seen me a lone Englishman on Greek ships. I was the radio man and they called me Marconi.

I knew that what I was doing was unique. It was like the French Foreign Legion of the sea. I lived on one ship, in one cabin, tramping around the world. I seemed to take some pleasure from the uniqueness of it, of being distant and alone, testing myself, and living life to the full, almost to the point of destruction. It was only when things weren't green any more, when I no longer felt the familiar thump of the engines and didn't even bother to look out of the porthole, that I gave it up and came home: but at that time, forty years ago, I was a long way from doing that.

My friend and mentor lived in Scranton, PA. He was my tutor in the creative writing course I'd enrolled in. I'd felt it growing as a deep need and one day in Philadelphia it became an imperative and I sent the forms in. I felt that I needed a purpose in life.

The assignments followed me everywhere: Panama, Valparaiso, Baltimore, Emden. We started off formally but as time passed and I sent off the regular analysis on set work and then completed writing assignments, his responses became warmer. I was flattered when he'd address me using my first name and expressed a view that he couldn't understand why I'd never tried to publish anything, why this or that article was ideal for a particular magazine, urging me on. I had the feeling that he was an older man who was vicariously enjoying my adventures.

I'd described the flight of millions of guano birds and chaos in the sky off the coast of Peru, of shooting hammerhead sharks in the Humboldt, of seeing dolphins, possibly in their thousands, stretching from the side of the ship outward to the horizon, all leaping in perfect unison and leaving splashes as though the sea had been raked by cannon fire. I told him of rolling to forty-five degrees in mid-Atlantic, hove-to and with two lifeboats gone, of avoiding icebergs in Hudson Bay and inching up the fogbound English Channel. I mentioned the woman in Baltimore who wanted my pet canary, my love affair with a girl in Chile, and running guns down there. I described the majestic Magellan Straits, Punta Arenas and Tierra del Fuego, and the balaclava knitted by my half-blind mother to keep her son warm. I told him I could hear the click of the needles, half plain, half purl.

Over the course of a year as I did my work on the elements of fiction, he was gaining an understanding of me and in his responses was urging me towards self-confidence. He had sensed something, recognising that I had a failing, a flaw. I kept holding back, feeling that I wasn't good enough and in subtle ways he tried to develop my confidence. I had no illusions about it. I saw it in my own father, who could have gone further than he did. It was almost a tacit agreement in our family that we knew we could achieve higher goals, but why worry, because that knowledge alone was sufficient in itself. My mentor, right to the end, gently urged me to reach further and to push the barrier.

We were close to the end of the two-year course when the regular assignment didn't arrive, and then I received a letter to say that he was ill. We went into drydock in Hoboken. NY, for a fortnight and I decided to go to Scranton by Greyhound. I phoned the college and was stunned to hear that he'd died of a heart attack. I asked to speak to the gentleman's wife and was given the phone number. When I phoned, a soft-voiced lady answered and when I introduced myself she said she knew me well and that I was her husband's 'wandering albatross'. She wept softly and after a pause we whispered goodbye. I sent her a silent prayer.

Forty years ago. Not long after that, I signed off and came home. All my writings and assignments came with me. I started a new life ashore and with it came new experiences. I started a career, got married and we raised a family. I continued writing and had a modicum of success, but the novel still eluded me. From time to time, I referred to my earlier writing, looking for inspiration, but in my mind would come the image of a kindly old man and I hear the soft weeping of his wife.

During the course of a transfer from one city to another, my writings were lost, a tea chest full. It wasn't immediately apparent and months went by until it dawned that the chest was gone, irretrievable: an irreparable loss. I grieved over it for a long time. It was like a lost anchor and for quite a while I was adrift.

I got over it, knowing that nothing was really lost. Everything I'd experienced was down there in the 'Deep Well'. My wife knew me well enough. At her urging, I took a year's leave and we went to Chile, where we rented a small farmhouse. She taught English and music to the children in the valley to support us, while I wrote.

Eventually, the novel was finished. That evening, I raised my glass of wine to the north and thanked my old friend. I called it *The Wandering Albatross*.

The Old Shepherd

The old man merged into the landscape, as a part of it. His weathered features were as craggy as the outcrop of the rock on which he was sitting.

It was quiet, with hardly any breeze, and the Salvation Jane around him was host to many bees, buzzing to and fro in the warm morning sunshine. He scanned the countryside as he had done a thousand times before, noting the things he loved, relating them to the seasons. Today, the hills absorbed the sunshine and the heat rose from the soil in a blue haze, folding over in deeper tones in the valleys in which there were pockets of trees, and there, always within his vision, the sheep grazed, moving slowly like a ground-hugging grey cloud.

The sun warmed him and he closed his eyes. 'Dreaming,' he thought, 'I'm always dreaming. What else is there to do?' How far back should he go? The war, slush, slime and chatter of machine guns. The Great Depression. He and Joan…trapping and living on rabbits. Hard days, but good. He had the company of a good woman.

He sighed and breathed deeply, feeling the slow, tightening fist of pain deep in his chest, like something alive. He gave a low growl-like groan. Then it was gone and he opened his eyes to see the blue sky again. 'Not good,' he thought. 'If only I had company.' He sighed again and noticed his feet in their heavy boot beside a bunch of daisies. 'Mustn't trample on you,' he said. Everything was precious.

His head nodded and he floated for a few moment. A slight movement in the corner of his vision made him raise his head. His faded blue eyes widened enquiringly, trying to focus on the shape of a woman. Out here? He must have been asleep for some time if she could approach without him noticing.

She was standing a metre or so away, watching him. 'Hello. Did I disturb you?' Her voice was soft. She seemed very gentle and calm.

'I was dreaming, dreaming of company,' he said. 'I must have gone into a deep sleep. The sun.'

'Here I am,' she smiled. 'I'm company.'

'But where are you from?' He looked around the empty countryside.

'I was walking and saw you sitting here.'

He looked at her and his fingers scratched the stubble on his chin. He was baffled, but yet he felt light-hearted and happy. He suddenly felt shy as he looked into her eyes. Her face was one of complete composure, with the hint of a smile playing around her lips.

She nodded, as though aware of his thoughts. 'Such a beautiful day,' she said. 'May I share your seat?'

'Please do.' He shifted to make room.

She placed her slender hands on her lap, hands that he could have covered in one of his large gnarled ones. She was too fair to be a country woman. Her hair was soft and white, like Joan's used to be.

'Tell me about yourself,' she invited him.

He laughed and shrugged his shoulders. 'Not much to say. I haven't added up to much. Nothing interesting really. Dull in fact.'

'Not to me,' she prompted.

'Well,' he paused and looked down at the daisies, touching them gently with the toe of his boot. 'I don't remember too far back. Hard days, the Flanders war, the Depression. I've been a sheep man all my life. Married once. Such good days, but all so long ago. Now I sit here, minding sheep, out to pasture, sort of. Won't be long before they ask me to leave. You see, they want to let the sheep go and move into cattle.'

'Such a pity,' she murmured.

'Business, you see,' he continued. 'Mr Carter, the boss, he's really a stockbroker in the big smoke. Sending cattle to Japan is the thing. I'm thankful he's kept me on. His father took me on a long time ago. Well, times change.'

'And you spend every day out here alone?'

'Yes, every day. There's no one to talk to really. I saw more of old man Carter but he passed on fifteen years ago. He had time to sit and talk, but the young boss only comes up from Sydney once a month. Brings his wife and kids. They love it, tearing here and there on horses, chasing goannas up trees and frightening the galahs. The sheep have got used to them. I like to see them, though. They grow like saplings, so fast.'

'You talk to them sometimes?'

His face brightened. 'Oh yes, I like that. They've changed. So polite. It's little Mike I like. He climbs the hill leading his pony, and stands gazing at me with his big brown eyes, like his grandpa. He's not shy and chatters on like a magpie, about his dog Taffie, his schooling and things. Nice young lad. He's the one most like his grandpa.' He gazed dreamily down the valley. 'The other two, Barry and Helen, they're fine. They sometimes climb up to see me, but it's funny, as kids grow older, they lose something. It's in the eyes. I hope Mike doesn't change too much.' His wrinkled hand resting on the rock trembled and she laid her own over it.

'It must be very lonely for you.'

He smiled. 'Can I tell you something?'

'Please do.'

'I talk to myself. I talk to the old boss. To young Mike. I say things to my wife. I tell her about the crutching and mulesing and how the boss used to join in. A lot more sheep in those days and I had all the responsibility. They were in my care and still are, making sure that they're safe. Keeping my eyes open. No company, no one to talk to.' He paused, allowing some thoughts to come forward. 'Not only that,' he looked straight into her eyes. Eyes that were kindly. Eyes that revealed the interest of one human being to another. 'I need someone. A woman with me. Someone soft and gentle to protect me. To talk to at night, to hold my hand, to be beside me in the dark and keep me warm, to be my friend.'

'And why didn't you look for such a woman?'

He shook his head. 'When Joan died twenty years ago, I became a sort of loner, spending more time in the hills.' He shrugged. 'Women like big comfortable kitchens to cook in, nice homes with carpets, places in which to bring up children. We never had kids. That was a sadness that lived with her until she died. I stayed away from towns and kept my own company. What did I have to offer? A stone shack, very basic. I'm just a shepherd.'

She smiled. 'History shows that simple shepherds have a lot to offer.'

He smiled and sadly shook his head. 'I have no education. I just know sheep. I like simple things, like saving a lamb on a freezing night, feeling its little mouth nibbling at my hand. Chasing foxes and dingoes away. The warmth and comfort of a fire with a raging storm outside.'

'I can imagine it. Doing good things. Sounds wonderful.'

'It does? Would you come and see me? Keep me company?'

'I would.'

'My shack is very rough.'

'Shall we go?' She lifted him gently by the elbow, but his legs were so weak that he wondered if he would make the distance.

'It's up there. We must climb a little higher,' he said, catching his breath.

'You can do it. I'll help you.'

His face softened. A tear ran down a craggy furrow in his cheek. It seemed harder to climb today, but with the woman beside him he knew he could make it.

Suddenly he stopped. 'Those little daisies. I'd like to pick you some.'

'I'd love them.'

They reached the hut and pushed the door open.

He felt very tired. 'Please look around,' he said between deep breaths. 'I think I'll just rest for a while…'

On the following morning, young Mike came scampering up the hill. The old shepherd wasn't sitting on his rock today. He paused and looked around. What a treat. He'd go inside and explore. He pushed the door open. The old man was asleep in his rocking chair. Mike gently pushed the chair, but the old man didn't waken. He had such a happy smile on his face, and in his hand there was a bunch of daisies.

The Regret

He was outside hanging out a trolley-load of laundry. It was his job, a part of the division of labour, and when it was dry he'd bring it in. His wife would complete the circle by sorting and putting everything away. Peace was maintained.

She called out and came through the screen door carrying the portable phone. 'Someone wants to talk to you. A man. He says he read the article about you in the paper. You're famous,' she added with a smile.

He'd received a number of calls, mainly from friends, congratulating him on winning the literary prize: a trophy and a sizeable cheque. He'd been pleased but not overly excited. The best bit was that he planned to use the money to buy a laptop, or, to be fair, his wife did, so that when they went caravanning he could continue writing. She was very thoughtful. She was very good at probing the Internet and finding the right product. It would have to be a Mac, an iBook.

He took the phone. 'Hello,' he said and waited for the expected comments.

They came in the measured tones of an elderly voice, spoken clearly and with continuity. There were no pauses, ums and ahs.

'Thanks very much,' he responded. 'As a matter of fact, I phoned the reporter and commented on how well he'd encapsulated what was virtually my entire life story.'

'He certainly did,' the man agreed. 'The mention of boarding schools in the Himalayas caught my interest. I'm an Oak Grove boy.'

There was an immediate bond. They were Himalayan schoolboys. They knew the sight of the Dehra Dun valley, the winding road that led up into the hills, the call of the barking deer, the clusters of rhododendrons, the oak trees from which catapult handles were crafted.

He smiled into the phone. 'I know it well. I went to Bala Hissar, up the road.' In his mind, he could visualise Lookout Rock, from which vantage point rocks and boulders could be hurled down onto the bend in the road that led up to Mussoorie.

'Ah, yes, I remember…unforgettable,' the man chuckled. 'We had to keep our backs hard up against the cliff face while the boulders rained down.'

They chatted away amiably. His name was Jim Pascoe and Archie introduced himself – Archie Green.

Jim had been back to two school reunions and was planning to go back in the following month for another. 'My last, probably…I'm ninety…'

'God,' Archie said involuntarily. 'I'm impressed…you sound great, quite chirpy. Hell, I'm seventy-seven… I get around okay but I wouldn't be game to go that far. We must meet.'

'Perhaps when I get back,' Jim said. 'I can then tell you all about it. I still drive. You're only about fifteen minutes away.'

'I'll get my brother over and we'll have a good old chat. A cup of char. When did you leave India?'

'Nineteen thirty-two,' Jim said.

'Jeez, I was just four then. Can you still speak the lingo?'

'Still enough to get around.'

'Incredible,' Archie said. 'Anyone going with you?'

'Yes, my son. He'll be coming up from Melbourne.'

'I'm glad,' Archie said with feeling. Christ, he thought to himself, how could Jim manage on a long flight? If you want to go the toilet, it's a long walk and just when you get there, some swine hops in and on goes the engaged light.

'I'll let you in on a secret, Archie,' he paused. 'I'm going because I must… I have something on my conscience and I have to resolve it,' he paused again. 'I don't know if you ever had a Langur fight, you know, when we met head-on with a troop of them?'

Immediately, Archie could see the muscled, grey-white bodies of ferocious black-faced baboons swinging down from the trees, rampant with aggression, mouths open and fangs bared showing vicious yellow teeth.

'Hell yes, Jim…dangerous, standing your ground as they came lower and lower. Full stretch, using ball bearings…'

'Exactly,' Jim broke in. 'It was all right if they let you pass, but you'd get the aggressive troop who'd urinate or poo on as you went below. That would be the signal for a fight. Full-on and we knew what to expect. Once, there were four of us and we had everything, ball bearings, marbles, river pebbles, and we were letting rip with full stretch, as you said. Down they came closer and closer, twenty, fifteen feet, murder in their eyes, taking the full force of direct hits, dodging… This big, muscled body was within ten feet of me preparing for a final launch, right on to me. It reared back on its legs and I gave it a full stretch but in that millisecond I saw a baby clutching the underbelly. The baby took the full force of the ball bearing and it fell to the ground. The mother screamed and came at me and in that instant Jack Bell hit her between the eyes. She was poleaxed.'

'Dead lucky!'

'You can say that again. The fight was over and we backed off, but I picked the baby up. The poor little thing was dead. I felt as sorry as hell. When we got back to school, I buried it under a tree. At the end of the year before we headed off on hols, I dug it up. The ants had done their work. I cleaned the little skull and polished it up. It's only about the size of a golf ball, a perfect little skull. As you know, we all had hobbies…egg collections, butterflies, some went for beetles and some even had dung collections…mine was skulls. I had a leopard, kar-kar, gooral, a big sambah skull, some cheetal heads and of course many birds.'

'You've still got the little monkey?'

'Almost eighty years now, Archie… I've got to take it back. I know the exact spot and I'll find my way there… I'll bury it and say a small prayer. It's the least I can do. I've lived with the deed for a long time… too long.'

'Good on you, Jim. A good thing to do. I often ask for forgiveness from whoever it is up there for all the cruelties I committed. The trouble is, we knew no different. It was a way of life. I tell you what, when you reach that spot with the jungle all silent around you, send up a prayer for me too.'

'I'll do that, Archie.'

'Thanks, Jim. We'll catch up when you get back. Have a good trip.'

Archie told his wife all about it.

She knew how he felt. She summed it all up with one word. 'Sad,' she said.

Three weeks later ,Archie got a phone call. It was a male voice and he introduced himself as Glen Pacoe. 'I'm sorry to tell you that the old man died a week ago…he told me…'

'Hell…I'm sorry…I really am,' Archie interrupted. 'What rotten luck! He was all set to go back.'

'Yes…he had a good run. He just went off in his sleep, just like that. He told me about you and I read the article… Also mentioned the little monkey skull. I've got it here on the table. It was beside his bed. I think he was fretting over it. I'm sorry I haven't phoned you but with the funeral arrangements and all that, I just didn't have time.'

'That's okay, Glen,' Archie said. 'I quite understand. What are you going to do? Still going over?'

'Yes, but later, not for the reunion. The airline has refunded Dad's fare under the circumstances but not mine. They've allowed me a later flight, whenever I want. I've never been to India, so I guess it would be good to make the effort, to see where he grew up, see the school…' His voice got husky. 'I'm going to miss the old fellow. I'll take the little skull with me. He told me the story and described where it happened. Here's my phone number if you want to have a chat.'

Archie jotted it down. He sat back in his Jason chair. He was quite stunned. Poor old beggar, he thought. He gave me his confidence, and his long-held secret.

He told his wife, with much regret in his voice. 'Poor old Jim. On so short a chat he gave me his full trust and confided in me. You know what…I think I should go. I should make the effort. What d'you reckon?'

She looked up from her book. 'I think you should…if Glen goes with you.'

Archie could almost see the gears meshing in her brain.

'Clothes…you have enough to sink a ship, so there's no problem there. It's quite exciting really. You know the language well and Glen doesn't, so you'll be a real help. You could even break the trip and stop off at Saharanpur, where you were born. Take the camera.' She stopped and then added with a cautionary tone, 'I hope you won't be too disappointed…a lot of changes.'

Ten days later, the 747 took off from Tullamarine. Archie and Glen were comfortably seated, sipping red wine.

Archie slipped his hand into his inside coat pocket to feel the little round shape in a velvet bag. It was about the fifth time he'd done it. Just making sure. His thoughts sped to old Jim. Silently he formed words in his mind – 'Don't worry, Jim, at least one of us is taking the little fellow home, and I'll say a prayer for both of us. I've been as guilty as you,' he thought ruefully.

The Loaf of Bread

Whenever I think of the *Andros Neptune*, I have warm feelings of nostalgia. She was a Greek tanker and I was her radio officer for five and a half years.

Built in 1942 in the United States at the height of the war, she was given the lovely name of the *Halls of Montezuma*. She survived all the U-boat hazards of the Atlantic and Pacific. When hostilities ceased, she went into dry dock in Hoboken, New York, for a complete and well needed refit, then changed hands and became the *Esso Cardiff* for a year or so. She was then bought by the Greek Goulandris group in 1950. They were from the island of Andros in the Aegean Sea, with a maritime tradition. Their main office was at 80 Broadway, New York.

She carried crude oil from the Persian Gulf to Europe or wherever the product was required. She was in Houston, Texas, when her disgruntled radio officer decided to sign off. He was a grumpy old Canadian and he and the Greeks couldn't get on.

I'd finished five and half years on the China Coast with China Navigation, returned to the UK, studied and got my first class PMG certificate. Much to the regret of my mother and father, who hadn't seen me for five years, I accepted the job of replacement. I was flown from London to Glasgow, across to Gander in Newfoundland, and down to New York.

While waiting for my flight down to Houston, I had the unexpected pleasure of meeting and having a pleasant chat with Mrs Roosevelt, wife of the former president of the USA. She happened to sit on the bench beside me. A very pleasant lady who was quite interested in my career path as a radio officer, and the adventures of being at sea.

My Eastern Airlines flight was called and I eventually got down to

Houston close to eleven p.m. and was met by the agent, who took me to the tanker base.

In the British Merchant Navy, the radio officer is traditionally called Sparks but when I went aboard the vessel, I was greeted by '*Gia sou Marconi*' by the crewman who helped with my baggage and took me to my cabin.

I was overwhelmed by the stench of crude oil and petrol in the tanker basin but soon got used to it. The Canadian gave me a very brief rundown on the radio equipment, and the next morning he was gone.

The medium and short wave receivers and transmitters were functional and adequate. However, there wasn't any radar. Which meant we were virtually blind. Fortunately, we had a direction finder facility which was useful in coastal areas.

In the UK when fellow radio officers heard I was going to join a Greek vessel, they wondered how I'd stand all the olive oil and greasy food, and jokingly warned me to be careful to not bend down when I saw a silver dollar on the deck.

But I found the Greeks to be a bunch of friendly blokes. No 'yes sir, no sir, three bags full sir', or concern for spit and polish, or uniforms. All the officers and crew were on a first-name basis and I was their Marconi. I showed my respect for the master of the vessel by calling him captain and he called me Richard. The radio room was my domain, the communication centre to the world outside.

For the first year, we followed constant horizons to our waiting cargo between the Persian Gulf and Europe, Lake Charles, Louisiana and Buenos Aires, then down to Punta Arena and through the magnificent Magellan Straits, up the west coast of South America and through Panama into the Carribean.

Then the Greeks made a crafty decision. We went to a dockyard in Nagasaki in Japan where the entire five-hundred-tonne bridge section was removed by massive cranes, the ship lengthened by forty metres, and the bridge replaced. Then the centre crude oil pipes were removed and replaced by eight hatches to carry iron ore, with the side tanks remaining for crude. She was now a multi-purpose vessel. It took three months to complete and I rented a small, comfortable Japanese unit with the traditional bamboo partitions and floor matting. A lovely, gentle Japanese girl from Nancy's bar came to live with me. We shared hot baths, delicate meals, warm sake and loving nights. We lived a dream. When the time came, it was a sad farewell.

We sailed to start the first leg of our contract to load our eight central hatches with iron ore in the new port of Huasco in northern Chile. A fertile valley extended from the coast up to the town of Vallenar. Ten thousand tonnes of iron ore came by rail from the mine at Centinella and poured into our hatches by conveyer belt. Chilean workers were all over the place.

To celebrate the start of the visits of the *Andros Neptune* to Huasco, there was a party for the local people. I met two English landowner families, the Wodehouses and Millies, who were naturalised Chilean citizens of long standing. They recognised me as a sailor far from home, and invited me to stay with them during the prolonged periods of loading. Their farm was situated in the good farming land and undulating hills of Vallenar. I would travel there along the rough road in a rickety old bus, laughingly called the *Bala,* meaning the Bullet.

The Wodehouses had a lovely young niece named Nena and we became good friends.

She had dark eyes and hair, a warm, inviting smile and a sense of humour. We went for long rides on horseback up the Vallenar Valley beside the river banks. I admired her horsemanship and sense of adventure. A romance was developing.

It was a great contract for the *Andos Neptune* and its Greek owners. We sailed up and down through the Panama Canal to Trenton mainly but occasionally across the Atlantic to Emden in Germany. There, I visited a cozy German bar, *Der Schwan*, the Swan, which was warm, softly lit and inviting.

During my regular visits, I met Hildegard, a lovely girl who became my companion. The heavy-set, unsmiling barman eventually acknowledged me with an unsmiling nod. Hildegard explained that he'd had a bad war, up on the Russian Front.

On one particular trip, I was returning to the ship after a three-week stay with the Wodehouses and Nena. I picked up the rackety old bus that spluttered and shook on its way.

On the way up the gangway, a man called out to me. He was tall and gangly, wearing a yellow safety helmet. He had deep-set tired eyes, with hollowed cheeks and a white stubble on his chin. 'Hello, Sparks,' he said.

It was a county accent which I couldn't place. He held out his hand and I shook it.

'Good to see you,' he added.

'English?' I asked.

The man nodded. 'Jack Wallace. Yes, but I was born here.'

The man's forlorn appearance touched a sympathetic chord. 'Come on board and have a coffee or something?'

Wallace looked around. 'OK, that'll be fine.'

I led him to the mess-room and asked the cook for a couple of cof-fees. Jack's manner was distressingly servile. His eyes seldom rested on my face. He was anxious to talk. His father, from Arsenal in London, had come out to Chile during the phosphate boom, along with hun-dreds of others. He'd married a Chilean woman with whom he'd had several children. I figured that his breeding placed him in the lower rungs of society, along with the Slavs and other immigrants who formed a minority. It was his lot to be designated to a subordinate role in any employment situation.

'A bit of a dump, this place,' he said. 'There's a big mine up north, Escondida. I've applied for a job there.' He ran a hand over the stubble on his face. 'Any chance of a loaf of bread?'

I was taken aback a bit. 'Well, sure. I'll have a look.' I went into the pantry, to the gauze-wired cupboard and found half a dozen second-hand loaves. I pulled one out. 'Not very fresh, I'm afraid. Yesterday's.'

'Oh, that'll be fine. Thanks, many thanks,' Jack said and in a quick movement held out his hand. 'Much appreciated.' He turned to go but paused. 'When you come back, maybe you could come and have a drink, meet the wife. She'd like that.' He nodded towards the shore. 'The house with a small veranda and some pot plants. A yellow door.'

I watched him go, holding the loaf against his thigh with the helmet covering it. A lost despairing soul.

We sailed and, in the traffic list from Amagansett/WSL, my call sign ELST came up. I fired up the shortwave transmitter, called WSL and he came back with the message from head office, 'Proceed Emden'. Good one. I'd see Hildegard again.

Weeks later, after a lousy Atlantic crossing, we came back to Huasco and I made the usual trip to stay at the Wodehouse farm, and Nena, and popped over to see Peggy and Bill Millie.

The time came for us to sail and I came back on the *Bala*. I made my way down the dusty street, avoiding a couple of ore-laden trucks. All the houses, simple wooden plank structures with iron roofs, were raised off the ground and were covered in a mixture of roadway limestone dust under a film of red iron ore powder. Windows and doorways were tightly shut. Just off the road was a short gravel path leading to a yellow door. I remembered Wallace mentioning it.

I stood still, the sun beating down on my head. Above the grating noises and rumbling of trucks moving, I could hear the haunting strains of Grieig's piano concerto coming from behind the door. I felt myself being enclosed in an envelope of pleasure and was drawn to the door.

I knocked and after a moment it was opened. A woman in a patterned cotton dress faced me. She was possibly in her mid-fifties, with a long, serious face, and quite tall. She looked weary, yet her face was unlined. The unbelted cotton dress was hanging on a spare frame and went right down to her ankles, with its low-cut neck exposing her collarbones. She was barefooted.

'Hello,' I said. 'Mrs Wallace?'

'Yes,' she nodded.

'I met your husband, Jack, last trip.' I paused and then nodded towards the sound of the music. 'Grieg. I just couldn't go past it. I love it.'

'Oh, yes, come in please. I understand.'

'Sorry to interrupt,' I said.

I followed her into a sparsely furnished room and she motioned me to a couch. There was silence as we both listened to the music.

She nodded and looked towards the gramophone. 'I find it very soothing. I close the door, shutting out the noise, curtains drawn and sitting in half darkness. Would you like a cup of tea?'

'That would be nice. Just one sugar, thanks.'

I sat back and let the music flow over me, conceived in the cold northern fjords of Norway. It had the power to work its magic right here in this flea-bitten Chilean port. Here, now, I was exactly where I wanted to be, in the company of this tired woman, in a refuge, in semi-darkness, two souls, strangers yet bonded together.

She brought me my tea and retreated to her chair. There was a moment of anticipation as the approaching climax came, and then, there it was, over.

She looked at me and ran a hand through her hair, a strand of which had come forward over the forehead. 'I never want it to end.'

'Yes, it stays with you,' I said. 'He was only a little fellow. The story goes that to be comfortable at the keyboard he'd sit on a big book, a volume by Beethoven.'

'How's your tea?' She smiled. 'I don't know your name.'

'Sorry,' I said. 'Richard. The tea's fine. Jack not around?'

'No, he's away on short leave, actually looking for a better job. He tried Escondida but there was nothing available, so he's trying Chuquicamata, a big copper mine, some say the biggest in the world.'

'I wish him luck,' I said.

She nodded. 'Yes,' she said with a wan smile and then closed her eyes and sighed. 'There's nothing here. It's depressing for both of us.' She paused. 'I'm sorry he asked you for a loaf of bread. I feel it was sort of demeaning, he shouldn't...'

I held up my hand. 'I understand.'

'Thank you. We have enough to get by, but that's not it. It's not about bread and butter. It's just, oh I don't know, a feeling of despair, moving from place to place.' She gave a soft laugh. 'Anglo-Chileans, not wanting to let go of that link. Jack still follows English football. Manchester are his favourite.'

'No friends? No other English people around?'

'Oh yes, a few here and there, but we don't mix.'

'Do you know the Wodehouse or Millie families?'

She nodded. 'I know of them, but I don't know them as such.'

I nodded. I felt at ease talking to this gentle, sad lady, her pragmatism, her acceptance of her lot.

'I'd better get back,' I said. 'Could I drop in some other time?'

'Yes, please do,' she held out her hand. I put both my hands out and took hers in them, letting it nestle there in the warmth of a gentle squeeze.

The Survivors

The man stood on the parapet of the castle, looking out at the wind-ruffled sea. He could feel her beside him. This was the kind of place she loved. Castles, churches and places of antiquity. In the past, castles like this had been the first line of defence of this embattled nation, behind which churches and the peasantry sheltered. Right here, on this moss-covered wall, bewhiskered Elizabethans, wearing doublets and square-toed shoes had manned swivel guns and sakers, raking the enemy with solid ball and whiffs of grape.

He was alone so he talked out aloud. 'I hope you can see all this,' he nodded, indicating the blue sea and Falmouth in the distance. He couldn't count the number of castles they'd visited over the years, all symbols of the murderous past of this tiny, beautiful island with its soft green fields and flowering hedgerows, as though centuries of spilt blood had nurtured the soil.

'There's a lovely house with a thatched roof you'd really like.' He could see a woman in the small front garden, wearing a print summer frock and a straw sunhat.

He thought for a while. Life had been so good until he lost her. He shook his head to drive off the image that seared his mind, but not before he once again saw the licking flames and smoke, chaos and panic in stalled Bangkok traffic, sirens in the distance while the hotel burned. He had heard it said, and believed it, that there was no disfigurement in heaven.

Life was like a lottery. The dice were rolled and your number came up. During the last years of their travels, he'd felt a shadow accompanying them. She'd laughed at his fears. 'There's only one philosophy,' he could remember her saying. 'Make the most of life while you can.'

At thirty-seven thousand feet, hurtling through the night, he'd imagine how cold it would be outside, falling, falling. In Asian hotels, he preferred suites on the lower floors. Lying in the darkness of a room, listening to the muted rumble of traffic below. he'd wonder if there were enough sheets to knot together to escape the flames creeping along the corridor. For a long time. these fearsome imaginings were just that, phantoms chased away by the light of dawn. Until it happened.

There was a muted hum in the air as he walked back from the castle. All the bees were making the most of the glorious sunshine, and coupled with this were the salty smell of the sea and the cries of seagulls, like lost souls flying to and fro in their endless searchings.

He approached the thatched cottage he'd seen from the parapet and paused to admire it. The lady in the garden straightened up and smiled. She had a fine, pale skin with a dusting of freckles. A slim, attractive woman, in her fifties, he imagined.

'Good morning,' he greeted her. 'A nice day.' It was an appealing little house, with all its bulges and leanings wrapped in ivy, leaving only the windows and doors free. 'My wife would have loved this.'

'Oh, she's not with you then?'

'I'm afraid not.' He looked into her enquiring eyes. 'I lost her… eighteen months ago. This,' he moved his gaze towards the sea, the horseshoe harbour with its marine craft, 'this is what she loved. We were here before, once, many years ago.'

'I'm so sorry,' she said. She looked at the man and put his age at about sixty. His blue eyes held hers and she sensed that in their silent appraisal there was a search for friendship. 'I've always loved the sea,' she paused, 'even though it can be so cruel.'

'Unforgiving,' he agreed. 'I spent many years at sea…a long time ago. A good life for a young man, but it's all gone. All those years and memories have faded into a blur. A pity.'

'I know what you mean. My husband was on the China coast.' She looked wistful for a moment, her blue eyes dark under the brim of her hat. 'Yes, I know perfectly what you mean, when I think of us as a young couple in Hong Kong.'

'My old stamping ground.' He gave a soft laugh. For the briefest moment, he could see the harbour, ships at anchor, black hulled and white superstructures. He came back. 'I can almost smell it,' he said. 'Well, I must press on. I've taken your time.'

'I'm going to make a cup of tea. Would you care to join me?'

He hesitated, sensing the shadow at his side. Then he looked at the gentle face with its hint of sadness in front of him. 'Thank you, I'd like that.'

It was pleasantly dim and cool inside, with shafts of sunlight streaming in from the windows. He stood with his back to the fireplace and mantelpiece, admiring the delicate mistiness of a Chinese mountain scene on a narrow, hanging scroll and the dull lustre of a Satsuma vase glinting from a shelf in the corner of the room.

He turned to briefly scan the photographs on the mantelpiece. He smiled as he felt the surge of instant recognition. He heard her coming with the rattling sounds of cups on a tray and looked at her her with the smile still on his face. She put the tray down and stood beside him.

'I should apologise,' he said. 'I mean, I had no right to,' he turned towards the photographs, 'but I saw ships and uniforms. Your husband, chief engineer?'

'Yes,' she said. 'Were you there?'

'Yes, I know all those ships. Some of these must have been taken from head office. I was with them for five years.'

She smiled. 'Come, do sit down. My husband was with the company until he retired.'

'Is that when you bought this house?'

'Yes, five years ago.' She paused for a moment and then carefully poured the tea. 'You're from Australia, I think? I went there many years ago, with my husband. It was so fresh. Like you, I have so many memories.'

'Yes, I'm travelling. Like a pilgrimage,' he replied. 'I haven't much to keep me at home.' He thought for a moment. 'My wife would have wanted me to carry on. Not get in a rut. Her philosophy was to make the most out of life.'

She was an attentive listener, her eyes scanning his face, drawing on all the information and inferences in his words. 'I think that what she said was very sensible.' She laid her hands on her lap, as though composing herself. 'How did you lose your wife?'

'Fire, in a hotel in Bangkok. The worst possible way!'

She put trembling fingers to her lips. 'I lost my husband the same way. Oh, I know how you feel! Such an awful waste. It was on the Falmouth ferry. Fire and panic, just here, no more than five hundred metres away,' she looked at him, showing the remembered anguish in her eyes.

He nodded in understanding. 'They say it helps to talk.'

'I know.' She sighed and closed her eyes. 'It's all here in my mind, the panic, my skirt on fire, Bill pushing and helping. There was a young woman with a baby. He made me jump.' There was a catch in her voice. 'Then an explosion, flames and the ferry heeled over.'

They sat in silence, her eyes occasionally straying to the mantelpiece.

'It's not easy being a survivor,' he said. 'I'm glad we've met, and talked. It does help, don't you think?'

'Yes,' she nodded. 'Are you here long?'

'As long as I like,' he smiled. 'We're old China hands, as it were. I'd like to come back, If I may?'

'Please do. I'd like that.' She smiled.

Waiting For a Sign

'You know,' Jane said, 'the biggest regret I have is that there was no chance to say goodbye to Mum. You know what I mean.' She paused, 'We always said we would.' She looked at me with eyes that sought understanding.

'I know,' I replied to this frequent expression of my wife's regret, 'but just think how lucky she was to go the way she did. Phht!' I clicked my finger. 'Gone, no pain. In the bath, flannel in her hand resting on her thigh, looking at the wall in front. A sudden blackness.'

'Oh, I know,' she responded, 'but you understand, it's been a year now. She could give me a sign.'

'You need to be patient, sweetheart,' I said. 'It may still happen,' I consoled her.

'I hope so. I still feel that she's close to me. I hope she approves of how I'm running her shop,' Jane said.

'You bet. She's up there, looking down and checking the stock. Leave her to it. Here we are on holiday, in Cornwall, a long way from Oz, and why? Because, as you've said, let's enjoy life while we can, while we're still fit. Not like the old girl, who exhausted herself with the shop. She became totally buggered. Didn't let up. Day after day, down to the the quay to Manly, the bus and then dragging herself up the stairs to her unit, and then the books. No wonder something went pop. Poor old chook,' I said fondly. 'Gone with no time to enjoy retirement. You've done the right thing, putting in a manager to run the shop. She left you a small fortune so you can enjoy yourself.'

The Hoppa bus taking us from Helston to Mevagissey pulled in at the stop and we got off, humping our backpacks. A couple of twists and turns down the narrow cobblestoned streets and we were outside an old Tudor house, the Spring Inn, at least three hundred years old, I reckoned. It had a definite lean to it.

I was just about to ring the small brass bell when the door opened and a slim, red-haired woman emerged and immediately flashed us a smile. Jane's koala T-shirt was hidden under a windcheater, so don't ask me how but she knew we were Australians. She reached out and impulsively squeezed my hand. Maybe it was the sight of an old backpacker and his slightly younger wife that made her take a shine to us.

'Australians, yes,' she nodded. 'We have a room upstairs, but really it's just a bit small. I think you'd be more comfortable at the Porbeagle Inn. They have better accommodation. It's not far from here. They're friends of mine. When you've settled in, come back here for a drink or two.'

We took her advice and later, when the sun was setting, casting its reflections on the water, we retraced our steps back to the pub. I had to duck my head to get safely under the dark aged beams that supported the building. The timbered floor of ancient polished oak was a bit irregular and squeaked with the pressure of each tread. A perfect pub atmosphere with the smell of ale, dark oak paneling, rows of bottles and glasses, polished horse brasses and gleaming pump handles to draw the beer.

Over a pint of Duchy Best bitter and a fluffy-duck, we got to know Viv, the red-haired owner and barmaid. It was early, so we were the only people in the bar and she was happy to talk.

She smoked like a chimney and was laughingly quite fatalistic about it. 'I'm forty now but I'll be gone by fifty-one, plus or minus, like my mother. When we're full, the whole room is in a haze of smoke. Can't escape and when the piano player comes in, the place fills up even more.'

I ordered another pint and glancing up made a note of where the Gents was located.

The outer door opened and a man and a woman came in and made their way to the bar. They had the stamp of travellers about them. Both were from Wales, on a short holiday, away from five kids. The woman, Kate, certainly didn't look like a mother of such a brood. She sipped her double Scotch contentedly, chatting happily, savouring her brief escape from domesticity. The husband was a bit dour, nursing a pint. He hadn't said a word.

Suddenly Viv said, 'I'm a medium. Is there another one here?'

'Not me, heavens!!' Jane spoke up.

'I am,' Kate said. 'And I could feel someone else too.'

We all listened intently as Viv and Kate talked.

'I have a Maori,' Viv said with a laugh. 'He sits right here.' She turned her head and looked over her right shoulder. 'Why a Maori, I don't know.'

I was intrigued. 'Literally, just sits there? A Maori face?' I said.

'Yes,' Viv replied. 'Quite friendly. Ugly little beggar.'

'I couldn't imagine it. A Maori, a Kiwi. A Druid, someone from the Stonhenge period, or an Elizabethan might have been appropriate.'

Viv and Kate were talking about their gifts. Kate ran a healing clinic and in response to Jane's questions produced a business card.

'My eldest son runs it,' Kate spoke and rolled her eyes. 'He really is gifted. Frightens me sometimes.'

Jane looked at me and nodded, questions in her eyes. She turned to both Viv and Kate and told them that her mother had died and how much she would like to make contact with her. She described how close they were.

I could see Kate's husband was getting restless. He said to her, 'Not now, you're on holiday.'

Kate ignored him, and smiled at Jane. She raised her glass. 'A double Scotch dulls one's senses, but I can try.' She turned to Jane. 'It may happen soon.'

Viv had been wiping the counter with a rag and suddenly stopped with a perplexed look on her face. She raised her hand, asking for silence and inclined her head. 'I can feel something. It's like hearing a knock on a front door and finding no one there when you check. It's like that.

A soft knocking. She leaned over and took Jane's hand. 'I think she's close by.'

An old man came in, got half a pint and went to the piano. He began to thump out old tunes like 'Blue Moon' and 'Roaming in the Gloaming'. This brought more tears to Jane's eyes. It reminded her of family times when her mother was alive. Her uncle played the piano at family gatherings, and they all sang together, with gusto, around the piano.

Viv stood still. She first looked at Kate, then turned to Jane, and placed her hand on her shoulder. She smiled. 'Your mother just told me to say "Goodbye".'

Jane smiled through her tears. 'That's what I wanted to hear.'

An Eventful Voyage

1955. I was the radio officer on a Greek tanker, the *Naxos*. The Greeks being clever, had converted her in Nagasaki to carry iron ore in eight centre hatches, leaving the side tanks for crude oil, making her a multipurpose vessel. They were also thrifty, doing without radar, but there was a direction finder loop, which allowed me to take bearings off land based beacons.

We sailed from Huasco in Chile with ten thousand tonnes of iron ore, destination Emden in Germany, seventeen days away. I had a girlfriend there, Hildegard.

The seas were calm off the Chilean and Peruvian coasts. We were watching thousands of guano birds and rafts of pelicans feeding off shoals of anchovy, and hammerhead sharks feasting. Passing through the Panama Canal was always a pleasure before entering the Atlantic, which on this occasion was calm.

It was a good trip until Lands End, when we entered the English Channel and were faced by a massive fog bank. Terrifying! A dense grey eerie mist. A congested maritime passage with vessels going both ways. Extreme danger with no radar to use as eyes. Visibility down to thirty metres.

We proceeded at slow speed. Men on the bow and deck officers on the bridge and out on the starboard and port wings, alert and estimating distance and speed of oncoming vessels as they blasted the air with their sirens, answered by us. Foghorns, some like low growls, others with distant moans like the grumblings of dinosaurs in some steamy primeval swamp.

Silence on the bridge, quiet breathing, eyes and ears alert as an estimated dozen vessels approached us, passing by unseen, just the thrashing sound of their props. I came up from the mess room with a hot toast and a hard-boiled egg in my hand and went onto the starboard wing.

There was a sudden shout of alarm from the men on the bow and within thirty seconds a huge shape emerged, lights on in the wheelhouse. There was instant panic as our siren blasted the air, answered almost simultaneously by his. The shouts of alarm changed rapidly into hoarse abuse, fists raised as they hurled the F word, '*Gamoto, gamoto*' at the oncoming vessel. It was a Turkish ship, the *Gundogumu*. '*Gaidaros, gaidoros*. Donkeys, donkeys,' they screamed, followed by a chorus of the ultimate insult, '*Malta yok, Malta yok*.' A hoarse chorus of abusive language came from the Turks. About forty feet separated us. Within seconds, his bow was abeam of ours. Then their wheelhouse came abeam of our wing and I hurled my egg and yelled with glee as it bounced off the shoulder of the crewman on the wheel. It was all over in about a dozen propeller thrusts. The clutching fear, the excitement, and then the huge bulk of the vessel throbbed away into the fog, pursued by the continued cursing from our ship. Enmity between Greeks and Turks went back centuries.

We all breathed sighs of relief but the captain and mate and other were still expressing their loathing of the Turks.

'What is *Malta yok*?' I asked.

'Ah, Marconi,' – they called me that because I was the radio man – '*Malta yok*,' and they began to laugh. 'When the Turks started their merchant marine fleet, they sent a ship out on a navigation exercise to find the island of Malta. The ship returned several days later to report that there was no Malta. That it didn't exist. That's how stupid they are. Stupid!'

Fogbound for twelve hours, we inched our way just off the Dutch coast, our course based on the direction finder readings I was taking from the Noord Hinder and Terschelling beacons. About six hours later, the wind picked up and a fierce North Sea storm swept in, driving the fog away. The ship began to pitch, bringing waves over the bow, covering the hatches and streaming away into the scuppers.

Using markers chained to the seabed to indicate the course, we entered the mine-free channel off the German coast. Mines had been laid on the sea floor during the Second World War but minesweepers had cleared them and pronounced the channel free of mines. Pitching into white caps and with reduced visibility, we pushed forward, heading towards the Ems. Marker buoy 19 was a few miles ahead, somewhere. Typical North Sea weather: heaving sea, visibility down to a few hundred yards, spray and swirling mist and a cloud base not far above the mast.

I left the radio room and climbed the stairs up to the bridge, using the handrail to steady myself. Everyone had heavy clothing on. I buttoned myself up and went onto the port wing, immediately buffeted by the wind. The captain, the third mate and the seaman on the wheel were occupied, staring through the windscreens. We were at slow speed, probing through the muck.

The chief mate followed me out to the wing. '*Poli kindonos*,' he worried. 'Big danger!'

There was a sudden shout, then a scream of alarm and scurrying feet as the captain rushed towards us, thrusting his hand out, pointing forward. 'MINE! MINE! *DEXIA DEXIA! GRIGORA!* PORT PORT FAST.'

The chief mate had rushed to the starboard wing and was shouting the opposite, '*ARISTERA! ARISTERA!* STARBOARD.'

There, dead ahead, about a hundred yards away, a big greenish- grey round ball, a sinister, silent menace, was rising and falling in the turbulent sea, shedding streams of water with its jutting horns clearly visible. I gripped the edge of the windbreak as the ship's bow began its laborious turn, first to port, stopping its swing, ploughing straight ahead, obeying the man on the wheel before it swung to starboard responding to the chief mMate's command.

'Jesus,' I thought, 'she's going to break her back.

'PORT,' then 'STARBOARD.'

Chaos, utter chaos, with ten thousand tonnes of crude awaiting the impact! A fireball crossed my mind.

The captain was literally jumping up and down, mouthing, spittle flying, willing his words to emerge. He gasped and then screamed again, abusing the wheelman in a torrent of Greek. *'ARISTERA, GAMOTO!'* The common F word!

Slowly, the mine came closer. It was a horrible-looking thing, sinister and full of lethal intent. Fifty yards and the slap of the sea against it as it rose and tumbled sideways. It came abeam of the bridge barely ten yards away, festooned with clinging seaweed, rising and falling, and drifted astern, with all of us holding our breath, afraid it would be sucked in towards the stern. There was a collective sigh of relief when it was clear.

'Marconi, please make report!' The captain was breathing heavily. *'Gamoto.'*

I slid down to the radio room, called Kiel, the nearest radio station on medium wave, and gave our position as approaching beacon 19 in the mine-free channel and reported the mine. About twenty minutes later, a high-speed German coastguard vessel came storming out of the mist ahead, gave two sharp 'Woop woop' blasts on its siren and the bridge officers waved in passing. A few minutes later, we heard a burst of machine gun fire, followed by another burst and then a boom as the mine exploded.

A mine-free channel? I shook my head. Touch and go. We could have gone down in a fiery ball with the iron ore dragging us down. The storm must have snapped the chains holding the mine to the seabed.

The event caused quite a sensation. The agent knew all about it, having heard from the police and naval authorities. When he boarded the ship that evening, he was as excited as a schoolboy. Eagerly, he asked questions, basking in the reflected glory as he grasped my hand, writing comments in his notebook. I gave him a brief description and then I began to enjoy myself, affected by the agent's enthusiasm. With a sense of fun, I began to embellish the story, describing the mine, adding clusters of barnacles and even closer proximity to the ship. I brought up the near collision with the Turkish ship, also other incidents, about once rolling to forty-five degrees in the Atlantic in the mother of all storms. My near-death experiences.

I met Hildegard, blonde and beautiful in the usual cosy, warm tavern, Der Schwan. Hugs and kisses. Even Erich, the usual taciturn barman gave me a nod and half smile. Hildegard once told me he had been on the Russian Front and had been a prisoner of the Russians. 'It was for him not a nice war.' She had a copy of the *Zeitung*. 'I see from the paper a story from your ship. Much danger. Boom! *Ganz gefahrlich.*' She paused for a moment then took a strand of her hair between her finger and thumb. 'Like this, a hair's breadth.' She was serious for a moment. 'I am afraid for you. So we must celebrate. We will go to my house and I will cook for you.'

We stopped at the Mercurio market and she made her selections getting excited at the sight of New Zealand lamb cutlets.

'We will have vodka and music.'

She cooked a lovely dinner. I stayed the night.

On the following morning, we hugged each other and said goodbye.

'You will come again?' she said.

'For sure,' I said. 'Your cooking is so good.'

'Is that all?' she answered with a smile.

Abdul

The year was 1914. Theodora Clara Houlihan was Northern Irish, a staunch Protestant, and had just turned nineteen. She had been a bride for only six weeks. Her husband Bert was away, driving a goods train down towards the Indian plains. She was alone in a cluster of Railway Colony houses in a remote area of Baluchistan on the North-west Frontier. It was hostile tribal territory subject to periodic raids by fierce, gun-happy Afriidis and Zakkakhels. A company of the Somerset Light Infantry and Gurkhas stationed nearby formed a protective garrison.

She was completely alone. The closest house was about thirty metres away, occupied by Driver Hall and his wife. Theodora was repairing a hole in the heel of a woollen sock. She had a fist-size, smooth river pebble inside the sock, to help mend it.

She looked through the window, her eyes scanning the rough path leading up to the house and then beyond to the low scrub-covered hills and the deep gullies. There was not a tree in sight. It was hostile country into which the North-western Railway was pushing, a logical necessity to bring troops up to the frontier. It was all part of the paranoia to block Czarist Imperial Russia's southern expansion. Britain had already fought two Afghan wars, deposing the Russian puppet and installing their own in Kabul.

She turned away and went towards the kitchen to make a cup of tea, but something, some movement in the distance, caught her eye. She blinked and concentrated. Down at the bottom of the path there was a figure, a tribesman dressed in the usual baggy trousers, rough shirt and dark waistcoat, and a flat woollen cap. His sandalled feet stirred the dust as he progressed. A spasm of fear ran through her. He wasn't carrying a gun but there was a knife in a scabbard at his waist. He was a young man, with a dark, beardless face. He was close to the house now at the foot of the veranda.

She quickly moved to the door and tried to close it but in her haste the push was not enough and the door bounced back a few inches. He was on the veranda and she could hear the drag of his sandals on the cement floor, coming closer and closer.

Her heart was thumping. He coughed, came closer to the door and cleared his throat. There was a pause and slowly the door was pushed in wider and wider. She was holding her breath, and her eyes were squeezed shut. She was terrified. His sandals slid forward and she smelt the heat of his body. She opened her eyes and she saw his sandalled foot just to her right. He turned to his left took a step forward and was in front of her. She gasped and swung the weighted sock hitting him on the temple. He staggered and fell to the floor, gave a groan and was silent.

Theodora fled from the house. She ran up the veranda steps of the Hall house, shouting, 'Help, help!'

Mrs Hall came out with her fingers to her lips. 'He's asleep,' she whispered.

Theodora told her what had happened. Mrs Hall ran down the hall and came back with her bleary-eyed husband, who was cradling a shot-gun.

They hurried to the house, where Mr Hall prodded the recumbent figure on the ground. He stirred, clutched his head and eased himself up, looking into the barrels of a shotgun. Hall spoke to him roughly in a mixture of Pushtu and Urdu. He began to cry, spluttering that he was looking for work, that's all – he was a Baluchi, he was aged eighteen, and his name was Abdul. He would work hard.

Hall summed it up. 'This fellow is a boy with camel dung still between his toes. Harmless really. He would be all right to employ as a bearer. He seems ready to learn, and could live in the servants quarters. When Bert come back from his current trip he could sort him out, and put the fear of God into him.'

Theodora felt sorry for this trembling young man and took him on as an apprentice cook. He was given an outhouse with simple but adequate facilities, with some blankets and a towel.

She began to give him simple cooking lessons and over the years he became a splendid cook, covering the full gamut of European cooking. He cooked curries of deer, wild duck, peafowl and partridge with superb skill, using fresh herbs, which he ground in a mortar and pestle.

Abdul became a member of the family and was with them for more than thirty years. The children remembered him fondly as being large and ready to laugh and had enough patience to tolerate them. His kitchen was his domain, smoky and warm – so warm in fact that eggs bought in the bazaar and left in a bag too long had hatched. He used to smoke a hookah to which he'd add some bhang, marble-sized pellets of gum from the poppy. It was an opiate and, after smoking it, he would see things, and would lay out saucers of milk for the 'small people' he could see. They heard him talking to them.

He became a loveable, harmless old retainer and he loved the children even though they made his life a misery sometimes. They would fire rifle rounds at the wall of his kitchen knowing it would dislodge soot onto his pans. But he left the chastisement to their mother.

When she asked him, very quietly, to cook a chicken curry, it was incumbent of him, being a Muslim, to cut the chicken's throat, which gave the children the horrors. In revenge, the children would set up a small home-made cannon, charge it with gunpowder, wads and small shot and set it up about three metres from his kitchen door. When they called him, he waddled out and would receive the charge in his belly. His clothing absorbed the charge, but it still made him mad, and he would call the memsahib. Then he watched with glee, after cutting switches from the mulberry tree, grinning happily while the children received their just dues from their mother.

He taught all the children to walk, patiently holding their little hands, and later how to ride their bikes. There were two girls and four boys. When in his mid-thirties, he would lift them up when they least expected it, and twirl them around his head, before putting them down again. He would pose as a wrestler, displaying his powerful body and arm muscles. They loved him, and his games.

There were times when he would simply disappear. The kitchen would be clean and empty. He'd return a fortnight later and after a severe scolding would resume his duties. Basuk, the second cook, was left to cope. During his absence, he would attend religious melas where millions of devotees would congregate to bathe in the holy waters of the mother of all rivers, the Ganges.

Mingling in the throng would be opportunists, charlatans, pickpockets and so called fakirs, who were semi-naked, with their bodies daubed with stripes of grey ash.

Abdul would set up a small stall providing simple meals, basically dal, rice and chappatis displayed on banana leaves, and a selection of sugar laden sweets, such as luddoos, pairas and gulabjamunas. Theodora and Bert assumed he was earning money to feed his bhang habit.

There were other times when he'd get drunk. One evening when Bert was away, just on dusk, Theodora saw some Indians carrying a large object hanging under a pole that rested on their shoulders. She first thought that someone had shot a pig, and sent it over. But it was actually Abdul, too drunk to walk.

With Bert constantly away down the line, driving his trains, it was Theodora who ran the household, ensuring the servants did their jobs, paying their salaries, looking after their health and welfare, including that of their children and sending them to hospital when necessary. At the same time, she gave birth to her own children. Her firstborn entered the world to the sound of cannons and other gunfire as the Railway Colony and the small town came under attack from local Afridis.

As the children grew up, Abdul began to show his years. He became a surrogate father, keeping an eye on them.

The routine for the children became familiar. They spent nine months in the Himalayas at the seven thousand foot level, followed by three months down on the plains with their parents. During that time, it was also routine for the whole family, including Abdul and Basuk, the assistant cook, to pack tents, foodstuff, guns and ammunition and camp beside the Sutlej River.

While Bert fished and caught mahseer and rahu, the girls swam and walked beside the river, and the boys hunted with their guns. They returned with duck, peafowl and partridge, which were all delivered to Abdul's tent, where he and and Basuk prepared the meals.

As the years passed, Abdul began to walk more slowly. He was noticeably grey-haired, and developed a small tremor in his hands. He spoke in a husky whisper. Basuk was doing a lot more of the cooking. And Bert and Theodora knew that Independence was just around the corner.

Lord Mountbatten divided the country in August 1947. It was the end of an era. There was a pause when the country and its millions of population went into a state of euphoria, but it didn't last.

Hindu and Muslim, families who had lived side by side for centuries changed their attitudes. Trainloads of Hindus left Pakistan and thousands of Muslims left for Pakistan. And then the killing began. Trains were ambushed, passengers were shot or hacked to death. Both sides were of equal blame. Nearly a million people died, although not a single British subject was harmed.

Bert and Theodora decided to join the exodus to England, as a small part of a massive diaspora. They would have preferred to stay, but there would be no employment for their children with the new Indianisation programme.

It was a very sad day when the whole family stood on the platform waiting for the train to take them to Delhi, where they would continue to Bombay, and then England. They were leaving behind the only way of life they had ever known. And, more importantly, the most important people in the lives of the children. Abdul, Basuk, the gardener and sweeper, with their wives and children, whom they had grown up with, played with, and talked to in Urdu. They were all members of a unique colonial family.

The children were weeping inconsolably, uncertain about the future, and realising that the past life, peopled by those around them would never return. And they would be without their beloved Abdul! The servants huddled together, but Abdul stood alone. He had never married.

The news sweeping through the country was of continuing animosity and murder. Bert and Theodora thought constantly of Abdul's safety. He was returning to his village in Baluchistan, and had been given three thousand rupees, which was the equivalent of three years' salary. Bert had arranged with friends to ensure his safe return to his village, probably by car. The other servants had also received large amounts to help them find new employment, and to re establish themselves.

There was a large group of railway staff, the chief of the porters, other drivers, shunters and firemen, all there to say goodbye to Bert, whom they respected as part of their railway brotherhood. He was the most senior driver, driving only the vice-regal specials. They formed a line and as they passed Bert and Theodora they stooped low to touch their shoes as gestures of complete respect. It was an honour rarely bestowed.

There was the rare gesture of Bert shaking hands with the servants, and Theodora sobbing as she hugged them all, almost collapsing as she held old Abdul. These actions were unprecedented.

It was thirty-four years since she had swung that river pebble.

For the servants, there were no more sahibs and memsahibs. For Bert, Theodore and the children, they were no longer part of a colonial family. They all were about to step into a new life.

Yabbies

'You're getting into a rut,' my wife had said as she prepared for another interstate trip. She'd wanted me to go with her, but she knew it was a forlorn hope.

'No thanks,' I'd said. 'I've done enough travelling in my time.' I was quite content, with no wish to visit the big smoke.

'Don't forget,' she'd added, 'the grandchildren will be coming to see you and they'll be staying the night, so try and be pleasant. They're boys, remember. You're a bit harsh sometimes.'

'What about their tucker?'

'Don't worry, Karen will fix all that, probably fish and chips.'

Beauty, I thought to myself, and while the cat's away, the mouse will play. Meat was virtually banned in the house, so I planned to cook an oxtail stew, nice and slow, for about ten hours so that the meat would just fall off the knuckle. Onions, potatoes, carrots, a good splash of home brew red, and Worcestershire sauce to make a nice gravy.

'Think of something…go fishing, the beach,' she continued. 'Yabbies. Why don't you try the swamp over there?'

My daughter phoned a day later to say the boys wouldn't be coming. They were going to see *Harry Potter*. Lovely!

A week had passed since my wife flew off. I was on the veranda sitting quietly, in a reflective mood, sampling a glass of red. I was enjoying the view of the Willunga hills, sloping down to Sellicks, and noticing the effect of the regreening programme as the former barren slopes were changing with dotted parcels of greenery, as thousands of trees took root. I was glad I'd retired here.

I felt I'd crammed a lot into my span of years: and yet, even now in old age when time was running out, there were still things to learn.

Computers, new technology, mind-boggling stuff. The grandchildren knew all about that. In my days, we had catapults and air guns, .22 rifles, and we fired at anything that moved.

Perhaps I had been a bit hard on the two boys when they came last time. 'Yabbies.' My wife's words came to me. I'd never caught one. Never. I'd been too busy over the past decades earning a living to have time to learn. Anyhow, they weren't coming now, but I thought I might as well try it. Perhaps I could teach them something when they visited next time. Not being country lads, I was sure they'd never caught a yabbie either.

I dozed off thinking of old times, of how I fell under the spell of the sun when I came out to Australia as a young man, tanned girls and beaches. Prawns were two and six a bag, oysters five shillings a dozen. Garfish and mullet were thought suitable only for the cat. It was a land of plenty.

The thought came back, nagging that I'd done nearly everything except catch a yabbie. It seemed that everyone else had. It was as if it was a national hobby and a passport to being a true Aussie. Easy, they said. Just chuck a line in with a bit of rotten meat on the end, or use a yabbie net, and you could have a good feed.

I got up to get another glass of red and felt a dull pain under my left arm and was a bit breathless.

I slept well but a fox woke me at about three a.m., barking around the house, sending a chill up my spine. He lived on the adjacent eighty-acre section, which was covered in Salvation Jane and had a swamp in the middle.

Later that day, I went to the butcher, and got a piece of liver and hung it in the sun to ripen; and an oxtail. In the late afternoon when feeding the alpacas, I felt a tightening in my chest. It only lasted about fifteen seconds but it stopped me in my tracks. I hung onto a post for a while and took deep breaths. It was enough to postpone my planned yabbie expedition for that evening.

I prepared the oxtail and using a slow cooker I let it simmer all through the night. Beautiful!

The following day was hot, again. After evening chores, I got the yabbie net, a small bucket and the stinking meat and tied it to the bottom of the mesh. I got my old shotgun out and pocketed a few shells: just in case, for snakes, and maybe the fox.

I went down through the weeds and when I got closer to the swamp, I saw a sagging electric fence, less than a metre off the ground. I wasn't going to touch it to check if it was active! My imagination began to work. Here we go, I thought: on my belly, inching forward and staring me in the face there'll be a big brown, coiled-up and ready to strike. I could see my body lying there for days. I dismissed the thought and hugging the ground inched forward, carefully sliding the gun ahead of me and then, oh, no! I felt a tightening in my chest, stronger and stronger, and a dull, diffused ache spread down my left arm. I wanted to reach in to pull this almost alive thing from inside me. I lay there taking deep breaths, not game to move. It eased off slowly and I felt fine but my brain was ringing alarm bells. The swamp lay ahead of me, ringed by a luxuriant green fringe of tall grass, so I crawled on and then carefully stood up.

I looked at the dark, deep water hiding its secrets. I threw the net in and decided to give it five minutes. A couple of black ducks came banking in to settle, saw me and climbed for height. Time was up and I pulled rapidly on the rope. What a thrill! There were four of them, thicker than my thumb, about the length of my hand, crawling all over the meat. They began to scatter and ineptly I tried grabbing them by their tails only to have them flick themselves out of my grip. I found two sticks and managed to hold them that way and dropped them into the bucket. I could feel my heart beating. I made three more casts and caught another five.

It was nearly dusk when I got home. I put the bucket under a running tap, clearing out the swamp mud. The elation had gone and the thrill of capturing something wild now had a tinge of sadness. I was committed to going ahead. I looked down at them, shying away from their fate. As a salve to my conscience, I put them in a plastic bag and then into the freezer, to help them to go to sleep.

They were survivors of some of the harshest conditions on earth, and I, the omnipotent one, was going to eat them. I boiled up a pot of water and when it was bubbling fiercely I did the deed, apologising as I dropped them in. I have to say that night I had a good feed of yabbie meat, vinegar, mayonnaise, black pepper, a nice green salad and a shiraz or two.

My wife came back the next day and I was happy to see her. I told her about the yabbies. She was pleased that my expedition had been a success but was sad for the poor creatures, and was very alarmed when I mentioned the chest pains. Without fail, I was to visit the doctor the next morning.

At six a.m., I got up to make the usual two cups of tea and got as far as the kitchen bench when my chest was crushed by a steady, relentless force. It was too much and down I went, on my knees. Somehow, I crawled or stumbled back to the bedroom and blurted out, 'Heart attack!'

I fell onto the bed. Tears ran from my eyes, not for myself but for her. Out of a deep sleep, she had to cope with it. I heard her phoning and it seemed like no time at all before the doctor was at my side, giving me morphine. The Aldinga ambulance boys came and cupped an oxygen mask over my face. They kept asking me what my pain level was, on a scale from one to ten. The tears kept coming from my eyes as I thought of all the problems my wife would have to face.

As they carried me out, I asked her to take a photograph. She began to protest but the ambulance boys gave me support.

'Why not, go ahead,' they said.

I think they were keen to keep me happy.

The ambulance drove off and I had a good receding view of the driveway through the tinted glass, and of all the trees I'd planted over the years. I wondered if I'd see it all again. I was hovering around level six but knew I was in good hands. It was a new experience. Yabbies the day before and a heart attack today. What next? I just felt so sorry that this might be my last journey with my life's companion, sitting here beside me. I wasn't afraid. What was that poem: 'ready to face that last dim misted trail, when eager eyes and pliant muscles fail, thinking of death as just another place to go, another road to walk, another land to know.'

Six months later, my wife already had me walking thirty minutes every day.

Jimmy

It was a glorious, sunny, midwinter day and I was pruning in the vineyard: a fifty-year-old patch of dry-grown Grenache. It was the lark above me, a tiny speck in the sky, singing away that reminded me of Jimmy, my canary. We were together for five years. My mind sped to distant parts: to the Chilean and Peruvian coasts, and Panama. Five years solid on one ship, one cabin, no leave, nothing, just wandering.

Here, south of Adelaide, surrounded by vineyards, I was as far as one could be from the areas I once frequented, a long time ago.

The lark ceased his trilling and came sliding out of sky, undercarriage down, wings aquiver, side slipping to earth a few rows away.

I was the radio officer, so they called me Marconi. It was a Greek-owned vessel, Liberian flag, with the head office in New York. The crew would go on leave and come back, and a year later, go again. They'd come back, fresh and relaxed from the Greek islands.

'Still here, Marconi?' they'd say.

Yes, Jimmy and I were still there. I was happy on the Chilean run. I had friends and a farm to go to when in port so going on leave wasn't an imperative. I knew that sooner or later I'd have to sign off. One couldn't go on forever. I kept putting it off. What about Jimmy? I couldn't take him with me.

He was a good sailor but like all of us he got tired in continuously heavy weather. He wouldn't sing then. He liked the southern leg, where it was warmer. It was a good run, carrying iron ore from Chile to Baltimore, up and down through the Panama Canal. Jimmy loved that, but I could sense that he didn't like Baltimore, probably because I didn't. That's where I committed the crime of breaking and entering. I only took what was mine, but technically I was in the wrong, had I been caught.

When 'deep sea', I used to keep him in his cage, or close the doors and let him get his exercise in the cabin and radio room, but in the Panama Canal with the jungle-covered banks sometimes barely thirty feet away, I'd let him go.

Frrp, frrp, frrp, he'd fly across to the heavy undergrowth, and as the engine room and aft section came abeam, he'd rejoin the ship and make his way back to the bridge. I always had the fear that he'd miss, but more than that was the danger he could have been taken by a fer de lance. They were bird-eating snakes and the canal was full of them.

We passed a Japanese vessel once in one of the narrow sections and Jimmy went across to say hello. The Japanese officers on the bridge with their high-peaked caps were giving their typical circular hand waves when he landed in the wheelhouse, did a few circles and came back. They laughed delightedly, hiding their teeth with cupped hands.

As I said, it was a good run. In Chile, I had a farm to go to, a fundo they called it, my own room, a horse, snipe shooting, and a girlfriend, Nena. I always took Jimmy with me. He loved it, particularly under the avocado tree. He'd sing happily, with his throat all puffed out and his whiskers vibrating.

He was terrified of earthquakes, and so was I. They were a daily occurrence. I didn't like the roar of these temblors coming up the valley. Jimmy could sense them minutes before. Dogs would bark, cattle would moan and the house would tremble.

Nena wanted Jimmy. She knew how much I loved that bird, so she wanted him, to prove that my love for her was greater.

The captain was running whisky, the chief engineer handled engine oils, grease and so on, and I was running guns. No problems, it was all worked out. At night, we'd heave to off the coast and the whisky would go over the side into fishing boats. The captain was making a fortune. He'd sit on the battery box in the radio room with his worry beads, running his fingers over them and saying over and over, 'One hundred thousand dollars!' Like a prayer.

For me, it was even simpler. I was dealing with the chief of customs, the *Jefe de Aduana*. It was as easy as pie. A shopping list would be placed under my pillow for single and double-barrelled shotguns, .44 under-lever carbines, plus ammunition. This was not to equip guerrilla groups but for resale down in Santiago, or so he said.

In Baltimore, at a gun deale'rs, I'd select the weapons and have them delivered to the ship. No questions asked. What you couldn't buy was a pistol or a catapult. A bazooka was okay.

The chief of customs also wanted Jimmy, for his daughter.

I told him Nena had priority. Besides, I couldn't see him caring too much. He drank copious amounts of really rough Chilean red, so rough that it left a stain around his mouth, almost granular in consistency comprising grapeseed and skins.

The most persistent, though, was the woman in Baltimore – Billie, who was from South Carolina. It was a break from the ship to spend time in her home, and she always welcomed a bottle of Old Granddad. She was all right in most respects, except that she was a racist. One evening as we passed a Greyhound depot, an old black American couple, stooped and travel-worn, shuffled up and asked for help. I immediately gave them a few dollars. She didn't like that and called me names. We had our disagreements, and I was no saint, but then, as I said, her home was comfortable, and with Southern fried chicken, a bottle of bourbon, the TV and a fire, well, what more could one ask for? Everything, except there wasn't much conversation.

I made the mistake of taking her onboard and right away she wanted Jimmy. Her letters would be waiting in Panama, always ending by asking about him and how he'd be better off ashore.

Down in Chile, over a succession of voyages, Nena and I made plans. I was going to sign off, come ashore and become a farmer. Then she changed her mind. I think she realised that I was too much of a gringo, too set in Anglo-Saxon ways, not flamboyant enough, a dull, dutiful lad who would be out of touch in the strutting, macho world. I guess she did herself, and me a favour. One thing was sure, my Jimmy was not going to stay in Chile.

I'd reached saturation point. I barely looked at the sea. I no longer sat on the bow, firing at sharks and at flying fish taking off at a tangent. Jimmy wasn't singing as much as he used to. We were both tired. I began thinking of home. I signed off in Baltimore.

The Greeks were crying, kissing me on both cheeks as I went down the gangway, with Jimmy in his cage. 'You'll be back, Marconi!' they called.

I kept on walking and didn't turn round.

We stayed with Billie for a few days and that's when she was most persistent and twisted my arm, when I was at a low ebb. I'd been with her, on and off, for more than a year and I guess I owed her something. I did it reluctantly. I said she could have him!

I made plans to go down to Florida to see my brother, but first I had to go to New York to sort things out. The company's head office was in Broadway.

Captain Raptakis, the super, stood up to meet me and shook my hand warmly. I had served longer than anyone else. 'You'll be back, Marconi,' he said.

'Never, captain,' I replied.

He reached for his tablets in the left-hand drawer and swallowed a couple. He was a man under stress, running a fleet. 'Anytime you like a job, anytime, anywhere in the world, you give me a call. I'll fly you.'

I knew he meant it.

'Now, where you want to go, London, then Australia?'

He pronounced it Londinon.

'No,' I replied. 'Florida for a few months. My brother is there.'

'All right, call me when you come back. I'll fix the repatriation.'

I went down to Florida and Jimmy was always on my mind during those months. He would have loved the warmth and sunshine. He would have been on the porch, not far from a tall date palm, watching the woodpeckers 'tok tokking' their way up and down, and seen the daily ritual as blue jays and orioles came to take unshelled peanuts held out to them.

The time came for me to leave and I made my way back to Baltimore. It was midday when I got to the house. No one was in. I went round to the back and looked into the kitchen, and saw him. He was a shadow of himself. He was sitting, absolutely forlorn, unmoving, and looking at nothing through the bars of his cage. He was in a dark corner, not even near a window. Before, he'd had the sea, the wind, sunshine, the canal, the farm. All gone. How could I leave America and be haunted by what I'd seen?

Using my coat as a pad, I smashed the windowpane and undid the door. I took him down and left quietly. I caught a Greyhound bus to New York. I was conscious of looking at the passing scene, and doing things for the last time.

I found a cheap hotel and made Jimmy comfortable. The next morning, Jimmy and I took a cab to see Raptakis. The Greek-American office girls left their desks to say hello to us. I knocked and went in.

'Marconi,' Raptakis said and sat back, looking at us.

I told him the story. 'Captain, you said you'd send me anywhere in the world?'

He nodded. '*Nai.*'

'And my canary?'

'Where to?' he said, without hesitation.

'To Florida, to my brother.'

'Not a problem,' he said.

He booked my passage to Southampton on the SS *United States*, leaving in two days' time.

'*Kalo taxidi*, bon voyage,' they all called as we left the office.

Jimmy went down to Florida the next day on a freight truck.

For me, a chapter ended when I sailed from New York. It had been a long haul and I was at last going home. I felt a lot happier, knowing that Jimmy would be fine.

Sop Kai Honeymoon

Richard found the Chiang Mai Trekking Office. He'd been told that Chiang Mai would be a lot cooler than Bangkok and here he was feeling the sweat trickling down his ribs. He met his trekking companions sitting in the cool inside. Two Danes, Maryann and Ole, and an Austrian girl, and they said their hellos, shaking hands. The Danes were affable and smiling but the Austrian girl, Anita, seemed a bit reserved.

She looked at him with a level gaze with no expression on her face. 'You are Australian, yes?' she asked.

'Yes,' he replied, puzzled by her blunt query and the lifting of her eyebrows. No hint of a smile.

She moved away to sit on a chair.

'Something wrong?' he asked.

She inclined her head and shrugged, searching for the right word. 'They make much noise. Are rude sometimes, I think. I have seen them in Europe.'

That was it, he thought. These globetrotting Continentals paid a sort of lip service in acknowledging the images of Australia and its people, the sun, the beaches, kangaroos and bronzed men, but locked behind their masks was the inherent feeling of superiority, of belonging to a much older culture. To make matters worse, at the back of his mind was the fact that some of the Aussies he'd seen here would do little to endear themselves to anyone. No doubt, at some stage, one of them or several had made a pass at her. She was pretty enough, but that's the risk girls take.

'You shouldn't travel alone,' he said.

'I had a friend. We went to India and China together.'

'What happened to him?' he queried.

She shook her head. 'She was Swiss. A friend from my work in hospital. She has gone home. You ask many questions.' Her last sentence was a definite rebuke.

The Danes muttered something and then said, with a sort of giggle, that they would try and buy some mosquito repellant. Richard thought that they were aware of his discomfort.

Fair enough. She sure was very matter of fact. Straight out. Cropped blonde hair and blue-eyed, nice figure. A backpacker, living off the smell of an oily rag. Probably been to Kathmandu, and into pot. It was the snob in him. He was at the posh Dusit Inn and she was probably at some seedy guest house. Travelling third class through India couldn't have been too choice, nor China for that matter.

Well, he was stuck with her and the two Danes for a week, kicking off tomorrow into the jungle and mountains. The Danes looked fit enough but Maryann was a smoker and she was bound to puff a bit on the slopes. Ole would be all right, and this one, Anita, was from mountain goat country anyway. Not bad legs.

He had no worries about himself. He was used to hard regular vineyard work.

The one thing they had in common was a sense of adventure. They had been drawn together from all parts of the world to Thailand, a rather nice kingdom. Not such a bunch of ning nongs after all. That was the consensus in the pub back home, that all these people north of Darwin were a bit sus, with their beady eyes on Oz. China was the one to watch. The only way to refute and modify these suspicions was to travel and open one's mind.

He'd flown in just a week ago, touching down at Don Muang airport, a revelation in itself, one of many ongoing ones. Within a day, he'd begun to regret that this holiday would have to end. Money no problem. He took to luxurious living, and being pampered by slim Thai ladies. A massage, a lap or two in the swimming pool, followed by a cold Singha beer in a beaded glass. As good as Fosters. After a few, he forgot all about high interest rates at home and a bedevilled economy. He was spending a bit of last year's grape cheque. Lucky he hadn't pulled out the old dry-grown Grenache and his five acres of Shiraz had been a bumper one.

'Your name is Richard, yes?' she said.

'*Ja*,' he grinned, and felt stupid. She didn't smile back.

'So, you speak German.'

'Oh, well, a word here and there.' He paused while forming a sentence. 'I don't like it when you and the Danes talk so much in German. I feel left out of it.'

'I will tell them,' she said sagely. 'It is not polite.'

They met at eight the following morning, Backpacks full plus other accoutrements. The heaviest item in Richard's pack was a bottle of Black Douglas Scotch. Ole mentioned that he had a bottle of cognac, along with several cameras in his bulging pack. He was editor of a Danish motor magazine. Maryann was attractive, tall, in her early forties. She was seldom without a cigarette in her hand.

Sanan, their young Thai guide, turned up in a minibus and with all their gear loaded, they set off. Sanan could have easily passed for a Viet Cong cadre. He just needed to be trailing an AK47 and have a banana leaf pouch full of rice tied to his belt. The assistant guide, Precha, was shy and spoke no English.

The Danes sat together so it seemed natural for Anita to sit beside Richard. It must have been the general air of excitement and anticipation that loosened their tongues as they described the various countries they'd visited, comparing them to Thailand. Richard was impressed when Anita told him she'd seen some of China's hospitals, been invited into the wards and had even seen a military burns unit. Well, this mob had certainly been around but strangely none of them wanted to continue to Oz. After the service they were getting in these Asian countries, he couldn't blame them.

They drove about sixty kilometres on a bitumen road, flanked by endless flooded paddy fields being prepared for this season's planting, dotted by water buffalos towing rudimentary ploughs. The bus began to climb steadily, negotiating tighter and tighter hairpin bends. Not bad having her thigh push against his as they went around corners. She smelt nice too, which knocked his theory that backpackers tended to pong a bit. They reached an altitude of about three thousand feet and the bus pulled up at Mae Sae, consisting of a parking area and a small store selling a range of basic products. At the back was the most important room, with a hole in the floor, the 'hong naam'.

Loaded up with backpacks, water bottles, sleeping bags, rain capes, the group crossed the road and in single file entered the jungle. Precha in the lead, followed by Anita and Richard, with Maryann, Ole and Sanan bringing up the rear. The transition was abrupt. The loose column snaked its way up, all leaning forward into the long interminable initial climb.

This was a test for Richard, and he was sure they were all making mental notes of the others' performance. That was what adventure was all about. An appraisal of one's abilities. He couldn't let the side down, no way, but the thought was there that four hours of this was going to be a bind.

There was an aura of pluck and determination around Anita as she moved ahead of him, her calf muscles taking the strain. She needed encouragement, he figured. He tested the words carefully, waited for an easy breath and said, 'Anita, *wie gehts?*'

She half turned and gave him a quick smile, '*Gut, danke.*'

The first and second pain thresholds from continuous hard exercise were reached and passed within the first half hour, and the lovely, almost addictive feeling of blood flooding the major muscles gave him a boost. By the time the crest of this hill was reached, they were all truly ready for a rest. Ahead lay serried ranks of even higher, jungle-clad, cloud-covered hills with corresponding deep, mist-shrouded valleys.

Maryann was especially grateful for the stop, and a convenient log on which to sit. Her lung power was diminished; nevertheless, she puffed contentedly on a cigarette. A pleasant, calm lady. She sighed and let rip a rapid stream of German, then laughed and coughed into her hand. 'What a beautiful thing,' she said and opened her arms to take in the whole scene, revelling in the experience of being so deep in a wild, remote environment.

Richard remembered from geography that Denmark was as flat as a pancake.

They began to descend, aiming for a small village on the valley floor, and an hour later in steady warm rain, wearing capes, the party filed into and out of the village of Pang Noi. Five bamboo huts, a toothless old man holding a homemade crossbow, and a sorrowful hog, tethered by a frayed rope, facing certain execution in due course. Thais love pork. Richard looked into its unblinking yellow-brown eyes and quickly averted his gaze. No hope.

Straightaway, a heavy climb awaited them and it wasn't long before Anita began to slow down. She'd take a big step and teeter there and he found himself just behind her, palms open wide to hold her, ready to push. They finally reached the crest, breathing hard.

Ahead lay a twisting, treacherous slope, a slippery track less than a metre wide, down the centre of which the rain came down in a torrent. Somewhere down there amidst the dense jungle thickets lay the village of Pa Kloy. Maryann and Ole led the group, slip sliding down, laughing and making light of it. Richard decided to go ahead of Anita, in case she fell. They came to a bend, came to a turn and down she went.

Her outflung leg hit his, pushing his left foot inwards, his centre of gravity was flung out and the weight of his backpack launched him to the left. Down he went, the slush and slime making it impossible for him to to retrieve his leg in time, and he fell heavily on it, tucked under him. He heard a muted click. He struggled up with helping hands under him, Sanan's and Anita's, then they slipped and he followed and fell with them, got up and fell again, and finally came to rest, covered in mud. A real circus.

'Jesus,' he breathed.

He expected to see a sharp blood-flecked bone protruding, but no, the left ankle was extremely tender to the touch. Anita was beside him kneeling in the mud, rain streaming down her face. She began rapidly conversing with Maryann and Ole as they gently probed the swelling ankle and traced the extent of it.

Anita rested her hand on his knee and squeezed it. 'So sorry. I am so sorry.' Tears welled into her eyes. 'Maybe, is broken.'

Maryann shook her head. 'I think not. Perhaps a bad sprain.'

Richard sat there in the stream, completely wet, wondering how a thing like this could have happened to him. 'To me, mate,' he muttered to himself.

Sanan produced a strip of cloth from somewhere and Anita used it as a bandage.

'So sorry,' she kept muttering. 'I am blaming myself.'

This was one for the books, sitting on his bum, in the mud, in the middle of the jungle. Sanan said that it was a good hour to the next village and elephant camp. Richard's mind shied away from the fact that it could have been a broken leg. No helicopters here.

With a bamboo pole for support, he began to hobble with Anita in front. It was slow progress and to keep his balance he sometimes had to use his injured foot. It was beginning to bulge out his shoe. He remembered coming to something that looked like a long, muddy ski slope, a very narrow shute confined by jungle growth, and thinking it was an impossibility. At the bottom stood Ole, in a mock pose, camera poised, leaning forward and waiting for a shot, urging him to go for it so that he could capture the action of a body hurtling down. It was this kind of joking that made a bit of a lark.

Richard eventually reached the base, forded a creek, struggled up a small hill and reached the village, muddy, soaked and in pain. Hot tea, a nip of whisky, another of cognac from Ole's bottle and a couple of painkillers from Anita's supply worked wonders. He averted his eyes as the women slipped into something dry. He reached for the whisky and got a disapproving look from Anita, a glance not missed by Sanan, who, when her back was turned, quickly poured a shot.

The elephant camp had moved, so another half hour walk was necessary.

Anita had gone ahead around a bend when he heard her calling excitedly. 'Richard, an elephant is coming.'

He heard the 'clack-cluck' of the carved teak bell around its neck, and commands of the mahout as the big, grey beast with ears flapping came in to view. Its small brown eyes of wisdom surveyed him. The camp was only a few minutes away. It was just a primitive thatched hut with a long a long bamboo bench, surrounded by elephant dung. Another elephant was standing nearby with a chain around its foot.

Anita led him through the dollops and sat him down carefully. He felt like squeezing her hand.

'Calls for a drink,' he said, and questioned her with his eyes.

'It is not good for you, too much.' She leaned over him, her chest almost in his face as she brought the bottle out from his backpack.

He took it from her and poured some into a small cup he had in his pocket. 'Try some, please.'

She gave him a sort of half smile and delicately sipped a small amount, some it dribbling down her chin. She opened her eyes wide and exhaled slowly as a slight flush crept into her face.

'See,' he chuckled, 'doesn't it make you feel good?'

He took the bottle from her, swallowed a nip and passed it to Maryann and Ole, who followed suit.

The Karen tribesmen soon prepared both elephants with their two-seater accommodation. Anita was nimble enough to clamber up, but for him it was like crawling up a slippery pole. He was led around to the front of the elephant's bulbous head and the trunk gently came around his waist and he was lifted up and put down beside her. She put an arm around his shoulder and settled him in. It was quite an experience. A subtle thrill sped through him.

Their elephant was named Pushegar, Golden Lion. He was a young tusker aged fourteen. They set off on a glorious ride at a slow, lumbering pace, right down the middle of a creek following the floor of a valley, looking up at sheer, jungle-clad hills on either side. Pushegar's mahout, sitting directly in front of them, talked to and scolded the animal constantly, directing him to move left or right, tickling the back of his ears with his bare toes, urging him to be careful, chiding him if he reached out to grab some succulent bamboo tips.

It was a splendid view from nine feet up, but a thought had entered his mind of a slip, a lurch, a clutch of fear, of their bodies tumbling, entwined down into a soft green jungle shroud, sun and sky glimpsed fleetingly through a leafy canopy, then obscured inexorably as in an eclipse by the ponderous, leathery five tons smothering weight, forever. They'd only just met. He squeezed her hand and erased the thought. He knew that he had a fertile imagination.

From time to time, Pushegar and his companion stopped to urinate or defecate, dropping dollops of barely digested mashed bamboo. All too frequently, their onward passage was punctuated by loud booms of flatulence.

His foot, by hanging down, drawing blood and swaying with the motion, was beginning to ache.

She noticed his occasional wince and patted her lap. 'Put your leg here, across,' she invited and brought her knees together.

'Very dirty, you sure?' he said.

'Come,' she nodded.

He eased himself sideways and brought his legs up and laid them across her thighs.

How had all this happened, he wondered. This serious, yet laughing girl, cradling his legs. A misty dream, going back to the moment when they first sat together in Chiang Mai, and now, so soon he couldn't look at her without feeling good inside.

Three hours later, they crested a hill and came down to the village of Pang Kaow Lam.

They moved into a hut, and Anita, anticipating his wishes, rummaged around in his backpack and pulled out some dry clothes and silently passed him the whisky.

'I need everything to face the *hong naam*. This helps,' he said and took a slug.

She looked into his face with a steady gaze, evaluating the logic of his statement and, after what seemed like an eternity, a small smile played around her lips. He felt like a patient in a hospital bed, comfortable and assured. He asked her to call Sanan and used his shoulder to hobble across to the *hong naam*, the usual hole in the ground within a square of hessian sacks.

When he came back, the matriarch of the family whose huts they were using approached him. She was a crinkly-eyed old lady with a pipe clenched between her tobacco-stained teeth. She smiled at Anita and him and nodded repeatedly, murmuring things as though giving her blessing. She began to mutter and blow on his foot and with brown sticklike fingers gently probed here and there, then suddenly took hold and began to pull, at which he let out a yell.

Apart from that, it was a very pleasant evening, after the rigours of the day, sitting in semi-darkness on rattan matting, backs against the bamboo wall, eating the white rice, chicken pieces and fried vegetables with chillies, Thai style, prepared by Sanan and Precha.

Sanan was a fund of information about Karen hill tribe customs. He said that soon, the old lady would prepare an opium pipe for her husband. He was sitting in a corner with a handmade muzzle-loader with a barrel so paper-thin that it must have been an old curtain rod. The whole thing was powdery with rust and would surely explode the next time the old fellow fired at a pig.

All four of them slept in one room, on sleeping bags to cushion the hard floor. Anita made him comfortable by putting a bundle of clothes under his foot to elevate it a bit. She looked nice in the dim, flickering light of a small kerosene wick, tousled hair and shadows playing across the planes of her face. He felt like kissing her. Too awkward to move. Why didn't she just lean over? A bloke had to make the first move. He fell asleep thinking about it. After the initial exhaustion had been satiated by a solid hour or two's sleep, he began a fitful turning, to ease his bottom, the left hip, right hip and back again, while frogs set up a cacophony of croaks at every dog bark and belly rumble of the elephants chained nearby.

At dawn, he heard Sanan moving about in the main room, preparing a fire for the morning tea and breakfast. He found himself staring upwards at the wisps of blue smoke, writhing and twisting up against the thatched ceiling, matching the tumbling of his thoughts as he listened to Anita's soft breathing beside him. Could things happen that fast, he wondered, and hoped. She was just a hand's breadth away. He eased himself onto his side and let his hand fall beside her head, his knuckled touching her hair. The regular pattern of her breathing stopped, then started again. The hunt was on and she knew she was being stalked. She gave a small yawn and a stretch. Her hand and arm emerged from the cocoon she was in and reached for the ceiling before dropping back beside his hand. His fingers touched hers and she drew his hand into the sleeping bag, snug and warm, letting it rest just above her breasts, and held it there. The regular pattern of her breathing resumed.

After breakfast, the party made its way to the fast-flowing Mae Taeng river, a fifteen-minute hobble away. The Karens had constructed a raft made of several thick bamboo poles lashed together. In the middle was a tripod onto which all the backpacks were tied. He wore a pair of shorts and was seated on one side of the tripod, allowing him to dangle his foot in the cool water. The foot was now a swollen, bluish-brown throbbing lump.

It was an exhilarating hour and a half trip, racing down smooth stretches of water between solid walls of jungle. Sighting white water ahead with rocks in midstream, seconds to go, quickly lining up by Sanan and Precha, judicious poling and whoosh, plunging down through the gate. They shot several rapids where white water rushed aboard and bubbled around his waist. He could hear Anita and Maryann squeal behind him.

They finally came to a long straight stretch and the small hamlet of Sop Kai lay ahead. A silent cheer welled up inside him. After the rush and turbulence of the river, there was a gradual calm and the raft steadied itself into a haven of peace. It was poled to the bank and came to rest, its task done.

Directly above them, about fifty feet up from the river, was a beautiful thatched house, high up on stilts with two sharply raked banana-fronded roofs covering a large platform, surrounded by a bamboo-trellised railing. Bathed in sunlight, as they were looking up they could see the inviting dark interior. He turned quickly and looked at Anita. Like him, she'd been looking at it, and as she caught his glance she gave him a big smile.

Below it was a small native garden, fenced with bamboo for protection. Apart from this partial clearing, there was the ever present mass of tropical growth, all around, a riot of fecundity that one could smell, tendril and creepers searching for a hold.

This was worth all the effort and pain of the past few days. The climb was steep and caused him problems, but the reward was great. Using their backpacks as support, they all lay back with eyes closed, letting their senses absorb the quiet and tranquillity of their surroundings: the shaded coolness of the big room, which allowed the unchecked passage of breeze, dense jungle around them and the murmuring river between them. Peace. They were Westerners, stunned by the simple beauty of the place.

Kham and his wife, Tien, were caretakers of the guest house and lived in a hut nearby, almost totally obscured by jungle. Kham sat on his haunches in front of the foot, blew steadily on it, closed his eyes and murmured Buddhist prayers, but there was no miracle. There was contentment all around, almost drug-like, and it was only the approach of Tien with a Thai meal of steamed rice, chicken, stir-fried greens and chillies that raised them from their lethargy. Dessert was a bunch of sugar bananas, plucked straight off the tree and placed on a carved tray decorated with flowers.

Maryann and Ole left later that afternoon. It was a touching farewell. They'd become good friends and had shared an unforgettable experience. Richard still felt like apologising for the incident but they wouldn't have any of it. 'Very brave,' they said. Ole shook his hand firmly and Maryann hugged him and gave him a kiss on the cheek. She muttered something to Anita in rapid German, and gave a soft chuckle.

They were alone. A sudden silence, a shyness. He felt as though a spell was being cast over him. He shook his head, unable to understand some of the emotions he felt. It was all new. Somehow he felt changed and better for it. Protectively, he put his arm over her shoulders and drew her close. This feminine, Continental girl, with no rough edges. He felt proud of her. She seemed to be putting her trust in him, and was he worthy of it?

That night, he and Anita slept in an inner room, under a mosquito net, with the bamboo floor softened by several blankets and their sleeping bags. She was aware of his difficulty with the throbbing foot. She leaned over and kissed him softly on the lips. Glorious. He savoured her soft breath and the gentle touch of her lips. His finger followed the outline of her face and she bit it as it touched her lips. He raised his head so that his mouth was almost touching her ear.

'I love you,' he whispered.

Her lips parted and he saw the gleam of her teeth as she smiled. They were lulled to sleep by the sounds of Sanan plucking at his guitar, singing softly as the river gurgled below.

Sanan woke them up next morning with a cup of tea, took one look at the foot and said, 'Oh, Richard, he broke.'

After breakfast, they sat in the sunshine and dreamed, enclosed in their own happy world. They felt privileged, knowing hey were sharing their deepest emotions in a paradise such as this. Like magic, their Western minds had been wiped clean, freed from the demands of that existence. Childlike, they sat, in a vast ocean of green, of many hues, so very far from the world they were used to.

Tien passed gracefully by, going down to the river to fish, smiling at them as if aware of their love.

Richard was starting to realise that what he had right here was the very essence of happiness. To be happy, there was no necessity for the superfluous trappings of the Western lifestyle. Here he had simple, clean shelter, basic food, natural beauty all around, and the love of a good woman. It was all so simple and he felt consumed by it.

Sadly, they would have to leave. Sanan said that a car was coming to take them to Chiang Mai hospital. It would be long trip on a narrow winding mountain road. It was part of the company's insurance policy.

He took Anita's hand and took it to his lips. 'I'm going to miss all this. I think we should come here again, go fishing with Tien, jungle walks with Kham, just…' He let the sentence hang, unwilling to finish the dream.

He felt her nodding beside him.

'I agree,' and she leaned over to kiss him.